THE TRAINING OF SOCKET GREENY

BOOK TWO

TONY BERTAUSKI

BERTAUSKI STARTER LIBRARY

Get the
BERTAUSKI STARTER LIBRARY
FREE!

---

bertauski.com

BOOK 2

THE TRAINING OF SOCKET GREENY

For the lost

PART I

When the student is ready, the teacher will appear.
Buddhist proverb

Weapons are forged in fire.
The hotter the flame, the sharper the edge.
Pon

1

———

Killing **Mother**

The narrow alley was filled with cups and newspapers, empty cans and bottles. It was sandwiched between two-story buildings with grimy windows glowing with yellowish light. One window was open on the second story, where curtains occasionally waved from an oscillating fan while I hid behind the lone dumpster.

I should've finished this mission by now.

Get to the window and save the victim, that was all it was. I was good at that. But nothing was that simple. Not anymore.

I was through the window on my first attempt and saw my mother tied to a chair with a faceless enemy behind her. I hesitated, only 0.04 of a second, plenty of time to watch him drag the sharp edge of his hand over her throat. You lose, Socket. Try again.

Control your emotions, Pon always preached. *Action must be decisive and pure. Never hesitate.*

Pon, the mentor of all mentors. With him, there's always a lesson. Even when you've watched your own mother choke on her blood a hundred times, there was a lesson.

Pon taught me how to think, how to move. And when the situation demanded it, he taught me how to kill. He designed my daily missions. In the beginning, they were simple, but now there were subtle traps, and traps within traps. Mind games. The solution wasn't straightforward. Not anymore.

Brute force is always the weakest response. Another lesson.

This mission wasn't about outmuscling an opponent, even though it looked like it on the surface. It was more about performing regardless of the situation. It was about focusing and seeing the course of action. It was about serving *life*. It was easy saving someone I didn't know. Saving my mother, that was like walking a tightrope. One wrong thought, and it was a thousand feet down.

Still, I should've been done hours ago.

The back of my arm was sticky and hot. A sharp slit ran down the back of my sleeve. I felt my skin flap open. A deep gash went through the muscle. One of the duplicates caught me on the last attempt. I disposed of the thing quickly—its generic head toppled down the steps—but it slashed on the way down and got me. *Bastard.*

Duplicates were human imitations. They did everything a human did—eat, sleep, shit, whatever—only they weren't human. At one time, they blended into society, intent on killing every last one of us. Now they were gone. But for some reason, I was still fighting duplicate mock-ups in training sessions; only now they were faceless.

They can look like you, me, or your mother, Pon would tell me. *The enemy has many faces.*

I pulled the wound open, probing for poison tips that sometimes broke off and slowly shut down the nervous system. I'd be laid up for weeks if that was the case, but the wound was clean. I put a medical patch over it, sealing the skin shut. The patch dispensed microscopic nanomechs that mimicked white blood cells. They would reattach muscles, rebuild skin cells and dull nerve endings. Basically a high-tech Band-Aid. In most cases, an imbedded device at the back of my neck would directly release nanomech cells, but I couldn't take the chance on it being slow. The patch was insurance I'd be good for tonight. If I ever finished.

Chute and Streeter were expecting me. I wondered if Chute would have her hair pulled back this time. The last time she had her hair down and wavy and even had on a little makeup.

I shook my head. Focus. My enemy was getting smarter. They learned from every attempt. They knew my tendencies, strengths and weaknesses. If my last attempt almost worked, it was guaranteed not to come close the next time. I was running out of options.

I pulled my aching legs under me. Another breath. Focus. Allow thoughts to fall away. Distractions to dissolve. The solution was in the moment. All that was needed was the space to allow it to be present.

Allow the unbroken circle, Pon would say. I wasn't sure what the hell that meant, but visualizing a circle calmed my mind. When there was nothing but the city sounds of distant traffic, I opened my eyes.

The moon was brighter.

The air was stiller.

I flicked open my gloved hand. A three-dimensional image of the alley illuminated in my palm. I hardly needed mapgear to know what was behind me, but preparation required vigilance and discipline. *Battles are won or lost before the first strike.* If I could note one more detail, it could make the difference.

A rat scurried from one building to the next. The enemies were on the roof, in the shadows and doorways. It wasn't realistic, duplicates weren't into guerilla warfare. When they existed, they were more about infiltration and deception, but Pon designed these missions. Don't question the master.

I stared at the mapgear image. Nothing new. I closed my eyes. Breathe in. Out.

Less is more. Pon repeated that one like a goddamn mantra. *The solution is always simple.*

Look at it from another angle. See all the possible solutions. If brute force is not the answer…

I reached for the evolver clubs on my belt. They unfolded—inside out—and wrapped around my hands and forearms like thin transparent gloves, fusing with my nervous system like a thousand needles, awaiting thought-command.

The enemy didn't know I was behind the dumpster, but they knew I was coming. They'd be expecting me to approach engulfed in a bubble shield, because that was what I'd done all day. If I didn't, they'd just shoot me on sight. With the shield, they had to engage me hand-to-hand. If they couldn't beat me that way, they'd just execute the captive.

I needed to be faster. Unpredictable.

Less is more.

With a thought, a translucent strand emerged from my fingertip. It snaked between the wall and dumpster, slithering to the far end of the alley, where the shadows were darkest in a broken doorway. Sweat stung my eyes. The evolver was stretched to its limits and shifted on my hand. Hundreds of nerve fusions broke away. I strained to maintain the thought-transmission.

I imagined a lanky form. Short and wiry. Bristly hair. Suspicious eyes. The tendril plumped in the doorway, taking a human shape. It occurred to me I was building Pon's body. Would it strike extra fear in the enemy's heart? Or did that just happen to me?

Weakness poured down my back like icy water. Indecipherable voices warbled in my head. I strained against the distraction. *Is that the enemy's thoughts, sending them out like static to distract me?* Of course, they were learning. They knew the distraction was as much a weapon as a dagger. I braced against the intrusion until the random thoughts subsided.

I redoubled my efforts, grinding my teeth. I focused on the end of the strand, holding the image in my mind until a body stood at the far end of the alley.

I took a moment to focus. I had to be quick. If this didn't work, it was going to hurt.

Breathe in.

Out.

A tranquil moment settled inside me, the silence a warrior experiences before certain death; the complete acceptance of the present moment filled me. *Live or die,* Pon says, *it does not matter when you serve the present moment. Embrace life* and *death.*

I was never quite sure if I could actually die during training. It could hurt like hell, but death? They wouldn't let me die, would they?

I focused some more.

In that silence, the evolver ripped from my arm and snapped down the alley toward the figure. Trash scattered in its path. The alley stirred to life. The enemy emerged from hiding, climbing from the roof and out of the shadows, strategically hemming the possible attacker into the corner.

My timing had to be perfect. I waited behind the dumpster, gripping my lone evolver-wrapped hand. I waited for the precise moment.

The figure in the doorway picked up the evolver club that slid to its feet. It glowed softly, illuminating the figure's aggressive posture. The enemy was careful. They stayed near the ground and climbed down the smooth walls like insects, watching. The figure would not escape, but they had to confirm its identity. My attack would be useless the moment they discovered it was a decoy. The figure slumped against the doorway, sliding to the ground like a drunk. The enemy reached for its face—

A bright whip blasted from my evolver-wrapped hand like a serpent's tongue and smacked around the railing outside the second-story window. It yanked me off the ground. Wind rushed into my face.

I twisted to avoid colliding with the railing and swung through the window, ripping through the curtains and careening over my mother's head with her captor's hand to her throat. I smashed into the far wall.

The whip released the railing and returned to my outstretched hand, immediately recoiling like a stiff-pointed lance. The sharpened tip pierced the enemy's forehead with a dull *ffthmp*. His head kicked back.

The enemy was colorless. Blue circuit fluid drained from the hole in its forehead. Its body crumpled like an empty sack. A red line appeared across my mother's throat.

But she didn't fall.

The line didn't gush, didn't drain her life. They had opened her throat a hundred times that day, but this time it didn't cut deep enough. Finally, she lived.

I fell over, couldn't breathe. A shifting in my back meant cracked ribs. Mother put her hands on me. Her expression of concern was accurate and realistic, but her touch was cold. In the distance, a wailing police siren faded.

A single curtain blew in the open window, then fell on the floor and melted. The walls turned white. The image of my mother melted like wax into the floor, followed by the walls. In seconds, I lay in the center of an ordinary white room.

"Mission complete," the room reported.

2

HOME ACHES

THE FLOOR WAS spongy and sterile, but the smell of the rotting dumpster was still hanging around. Pain spread across my ribs like claws. *Not tonight. I can't be laid up tonight.*

The room was empty, except for the faceless enemy lying next to me, a gaping hole between the eyes. I touched the thing's forehead. I could mentally scan the thing, but direct touch would allow me to experience its thoughts while I drained its life force. It wasn't real, so it wasn't murder.

Those things were just fabrications of the training room, designed to be exactly like a duplicated human. A duplicate of a duplicate. I always touched them when a mission ended to get insight into their motivation. Why did they want to live? Because they were copies of humans? Because they were self-centered? But each time I drained one, all I saw was programming to destroy humans and multiply. Was there anything else? Did they just want to feel real?

A SIX-FOOT SILVER humanoid walked into the room, his plum-colored overcoat waving around his knees, his physique chiseled. He was similar to a duplicate, thinking with artificial intelligence, but he served the Paladin Nation. It contradicted our mission, but I wasn't going to argue. If humans were more like Spindle, the world would be a better place.

"Congratulations, Master Socket!" Spindle had no face, just a textured surface with a single eyelight. "You have completed the mission with near perfection. The diversion was effective and your elimination of the abductor flawless. Trainer Pon will be very pleased."

Spindle's naked foot was a perfect replication of a human foot dipped in molten silver. He slid his hand over my ribs, his fingertips emitting healing vibrations. Warmth seeped beneath my skin.

"You have fractured two ribs. I will stimulate healing to assuage your discomfort, but I recommend we go to the infirmary for deep penetration—"

A pair of boots stepped quietly next to Spindle. Pon was no taller than me, slightly lanky. His skin was brown, his hair a shore of stubble. A thin scar curved beneath his jaw, starting at his left ear and curling under his chin. Some Paladins say he destroyed twenty enemies in hand-to-hand, that he cheated death by holding his throat together while he finished the last one. But no one knew for sure. No one knew anything about Pon.

I struggled to my hands and knees, stifling a groan.

"It is highly recommended you rest before standing," Spindle said.

My vision blurred, but I stood anyway. Pon watched Spindle press his hand against my ribs. The spot was already feeling better. The bright eyelight that rotated on his featureless faceplate focused on the medical patch oozing on my arm. Dark blue sparkled on his face.

"That needs medical attention," Spindle said.

"It can wait," I replied.

I felt like I'd survived a stampede. I stopped breathing to avoid wincing, but hiding pain from Pon was pointless. I could pretend like it didn't hurt all I wanted, smile like I was top-notch, but he would know just by looking at me. I let my breath rattle out, grimaced, and stopped pretending.

Pon paced around me while Spindle's hands radiated warmth. I wanted to shake him off, but it felt too good. I needed it. Pon intentionally let his almond-shaped eyes fall on my bandaged arm, a slight curl on the corner of his lips.

"Well done, cadet," he said. "You saved your mother on the one hundred thirty-fifth attempt." He stopped in front of me and let the smile spread to the other side of his mouth. "Well done, indeed."

"Trainer Pon," Spindle said, raising his hand, "the exercise was completed faster than any previously recorded attempt—"

It only took a look and Spindle stepped back. Pon's presence spoke clearly.

"I want a fully detailed synopsis of each attempt," Pon said. "All one hundred thirty-five of them. Have it done in full animated reenactment with an analysis of each failure. You will walk me through each one."

"I have a break tonight. I'm going home."

Home? He didn't have to say it, the expression did it clearly enough. It was the tension along his jaws. But I was going home whether he liked it or not. I hadn't been there in months. He could put a stop to it, could make me stay, require me to analyze every goddamn failed attempt so I could learn, learn, learn and train until my ass was chapped. But if he made me stay, he'd have to deal with my mother. An assassin like Pon knew how to pick his battles.

He looked to the floor and began to pace again. "Would your father failed to have saved your mother?" he asked. "Would he have failed *134 times*?"

"I'm not my father."

"That doesn't answer the question."

I met his stare as he came around. "I am who I am."

"You don't know who you are, cadet."

He locked his hands behind his back, awaiting a response. I gave him a response, but not in words. I was fully present, centering my awareness in the core of my stomach. I could not make myself be anything but what I was. But who was I? I showed him. *I am now.*

He narrowed his eyes. The atmosphere intensified. He sucked his breath between his teeth. Perhaps he was considering a discussion with Mother after all; have me train another three months before going home. Hell, if he got his way, I'd never see home again. The guy lived for this shit. Not me. I still had a life and a home I wanted to see. I had Chute.

He stopped in front of me. "The synopsis is due in forty-eight hours."

I nodded. He nodded back, just a slight tip of his chin. A slow blink. He paced behind me and then his quiet footsteps fell silent. The tension in the air suddenly evaporated. I turned. Pon was gone, leaving as mysteriously as he appeared.

I PULLED at the bottom of my shirt and felt my ribs shift. "Help me with my shirt, will you, Spindle?"

"It is advisable to cool down." He put his hand on my forehead. "Your energy levels are near exhaustion. You have been in this mission for over seven hours and you have not eaten nor rested."

"I'll grab a snack on the way."

"You cannot maintain this schedule, Master Socket."

"So far, so good." I tugged on my shirt. "A little help?"

Spindle pulled the shirt over my head. I wiped my sweaty face with the shirt, threw it over my shoulder and started for the dim archway on the wall. While Pon got around through some mysterious network of hidden tunnels, the rest of us still used the leapers.

"If I may ask," Spindle said, marching with me, "what are your plans for tonight?"

"I don't know." I stopped at the archway. "You coming?"

"Home?" Spindle's face lit up. "Out in public?"

"I was referring to the locker room but, sure, if you can get permission." *He won't.*

THE SHOWER RAINED from the ceiling, running over my shoulders, over the bruises and scars and cuts. Spindle stood around the corner, still talking. He used to stand in the shower with me, but that had to stop. He wasn't human, but still.

"Trainer Pon wants to remind you that your Realization Trial is only a month away." His voice was muffled. "He would like you to take your training more seriously."

I stuck my head out. "I'm sorry, what'd you just say?"

"Your Realization Trial is only a month away."

"No, the other part."

"To take your training more seriously?"

I stepped out. Water puddled around my feet. Spindle's eyelight spun away. I was about to say something. Take my training seriously was Pon's little jab to remind me that I wasn't done training. He just wanted to see if I'd react to the criticism, a lesson for the road. *Don't react. Always respond.*

I went back to the shower and rinsed my hair. "Tell him I'll be here in the morning."

"Very well."

Spindle continued with his list of things-to-do while steam filled the shower room and water trickled into the drain. I imagined I was in a cloud where no one could find me. Inside the Garrison training facility, someone was always watching. Always judging. Sometimes I just wanted to be normal. Nothing about living inside a mountainous facility was normal. I didn't choose this life, it chose me. Still, I needed to get away from it or I'd go insane. If Pon didn't kill me first.

I called the water off. Warm air filtered through the room. Spindle's arm appeared from around the corner with a towel. I wrapped it around my waist.

"May I ask what your plans are tonight?" he asked.

"The Charleston Squall tagghet season is opening tonight."

"They have already established a professional team?"

"It's minor league."

"And will you be meeting Master Streeter?"

"Yep."

"Your girlfriend, Master Chute, she will be present, as well?"

Girlfriend. I sat in front of my closet and wrapped my hair back. My stomach fluttered. Spindle asked about them every day. Wasn't sure if he missed them or he just sympathized. He knew how much they meant to me. It wasn't easy being in the present moment when she was so far away.

I pulled on my shorts and reached into the closet. Black pants, white shirt and a tie were on a hanger.

"What's this?"

"I assumed you would like to look nice for your friends, so I took the liberty of having dress clothes sent up."

I ran my fingers down the tie and couldn't remember if I had ever worn one. Wouldn't even know how to knot one. There was no way I was going to blend into the crowd. And in public, the number one rule was to blend in, don't draw attention. *Be invisible.*

"Thanks, Spindle," I said. "You have great taste, but could you have a servy bring up jeans and a black T-shirt?"

"Certainly, Master Socket."

I let go of the tie, noticing the scars crisscrossing my arms. "Could you also have a long-sleeve button-down shirt sent up, too?"

"It is eighty-five degrees in Charleston, South Carolina."

"I'll leave it unbuttoned."

A large, spherical servy floated into the room, holding a stack of clothes in elastic arms emerging from its otherwise generic body. Its eyelight rotated around its cue-ball form and fixed on me.

The clothes felt good. *Normal.* It had been a long time since I felt cotton. Most of the time, it was sweat-wicking armorcloth that resisted impact like metal. I saw myself in the mirror and pulled my hair back then brushed the front of my shirt and tugged the sleeves down. I was more nervous about going home than facing a faceless flame-throwing agent of death.

"You look wonderful." Spindle fussed with my collar, smoothing out wrinkles and pushing stray hair off my face. He stepped back, looking at my left side then my right. He tugged on my shirt, wiped my sleeve—

"I'm not going to prom, Spindle."

"Yes, well, you want to look your best." He stepped back for one last look; his faceplate was very bright. "You are due for a short meeting with the commander before you leave."

"Ooooh, that." I actually thought maybe he'd forget that, not that he ever forgot anything.

"It will not take long." Spindle clasped his hands together. "And before you go to South Carolina, may I remind you of public policy?"

"Blend in, I know."

"As a cadet, you are not allowed to use your abilities in public."

"Unless I have to."

Spindle's face appeared muddled with color. "I do not believe that is part of the policy, Master Socket."

"It should be."

"Also be aware that you may contact me for assistance at any time."

Assistance? Spindle was virtually connected with my vital signs. At all times, he knew my pulse, my blood pressure, if I was asleep or if I was taking a shit. It was a lifeline. If the signal faded, he would assume there was trouble and come for me, so there was no need to call for assistance. He knew all this, but he still wanted me to know I could call.

He followed me to the leaper. "You are driving?" he asked.

"I am."

"May I remind you of the driving policy?"

"You may not." I stepped into the leaper and left him in the locker room. Spindle's voice faded quickly.

3

—————

Chilled

I stopped by my mother's office just to see her. The thoughts of her gagging on her spurting jugular were still vivid. Even though it was just an image composed of clayey, cellular nanomechs, it wasn't easy to forget. So I looked in on her, confirmed she was alive and breathing, even looked at her neck. I'd sleep better.

I went to the platform, a half circle that jutted out from a cliff wall without a railing. It was high above the tropical forest of the manmade Preserve, a private jungle carved from the isolated mountains of the Garrison. We weren't on any map, nor were we accessible to the public by automobile, helicopter or mountain climber. I knew we were nowhere near a tropical climate, that was why the Preserve was enclosed with an invisible ceiling that covered the entire 5.2 square miles. From the platform's vantage point, I could see to the other side, where it was enclosed with a similar cliff, and in between it was all trees. And below the trees there were trails and streams and creatures from all over the world and, in some cases, other planets.

An enormous tree stood out in the middle, different from all the rest because it was barren of leaves. Its monstrous limbs were like arthritic fingers reaching for the sky, and on those limbs were the off-world grimmets: small bat-like dragony creatures no bigger than a sparrow with tails as long as a possum's. It would be impossible to see them from the platform, but the grimmets pulsated with color. Some were burnt orange, others were sunshine yellow or plum purple or jet black. Like a living rainbow.

Maybe I wouldn't notice them on the tree if I couldn't feel them. The grimmets were playful; they would laugh at anything. They were also powerful, and we shared a special bond. Our energies gyrated like time and space didn't exist. They knew when I was sad, tired, or bored, similar to the lifeline I had with Spindle.

That tree was where I met Pivot for the first time. It had been over a year since I'd seen him sitting at the base of the grimmet tree, but it seemed like yesterday. Long sandy hair, native tan, and dead eyes. He was physically blind, but he saw better with his mind than anyone saw with eyes. Sometimes, I wondered if he was even human. If it wasn't for him, I wouldn't be here. He saved me when I first arrived at the Garrison. He showed me a purpose to the Paladin life that, quite frankly, I wasn't all jazzed up about. It wasn't anything he said, it was just the way he felt. His presence. No words needed.

But Pivot wasn't around anymore. He left, and no one knew where. Sometimes I felt his presence, that sense of security, like a warm blanket. Occasionally, I'd turn around and catch a glimpse of something and swear it was him, but it never materialized into anything real. Pivot was such a psychic master that he could be right in front of you and make you believe he wasn't there. Suppose he was doing the same thing to me. Maybe he was from another planet like the grimmets.

"Ah, there he is." Commander Diggs, a hard-faced man with short-clipped gray hair, stepped onto the platform.

I turned at attention. Another high-ranking official walked with the commander, along with two escorts. They wore similar uniforms with a horizontal red stripe above the right breast that signified their training facility. I hated all the military bullshit, the saluting and ranking and arrogance that sometimes came with it, but I went with the flow. To run a society this powerful, there had to be order.

The commander squeezed my shoulder, his smile creasing his leathery complexion. "Cadet Socket," he said gruffly, "this is Chief Commander."

"Chief Com," I said.

He nodded slowly, as if to say *at ease* but not really. His hair was short and his nose flat. His eyes were especially relaxed. His mind tingled around me, feeling my psychic structure like a dog sniffing another dog's ass. I tensed, but remained open. Closing down to someone of his status was considered an insult. But to remain fully open wasn't good, either. *Always be ready.*

Chief Com stepped slowly forward while the others remained still. His escorts looked more like assassins, their eyes barely slits and their mouths equally grim. Chief Com closed in on my personal space. My heels caught the edge of the platform and a magnetic field pushed back.

"How are you, cadet?" His voice was hypnotic, pleasantly reverberant.

"Doing well, Chief Com."

"You may address me as Com."

"Com." I nodded respectfully.

"Are you familiar with me?"

Com, overseer of the Paladin Nation's most successful training facility. More cadets graduated under his tutelage than all the other facilities combined. If the math was done right, he was responsible for nearly a third of the Paladins' population today. Without Com, duplicated humans would be crawling all over the planet like cockroaches.

He stayed close to me and applied a bit more psychic pressure. I stiffened this time. He was testing me now, seeing how I'd react to standing at the edge of the platform while being prodded. He'd heard about me, now he just wanted a taste of what I was made of. A cold chill that poured down my neck during training started again. *Shit!*

This time I saw things. Images appeared.

I saw weapons flash.

Pon's sweaty face, bruised and bloody. His body lying still.

A drip of sweat ran down my cheek. I clenched my fists, fingernails digging into my palms, and beat back the chilly sensation and the images it brought. And then it was gone.

Com didn't seem to notice I checked out for a second. He stepped back, satisfied, and cupped his hands behind his back. "Your preliminary training scores are exceptional, cadet. I was touring your facilities and, while I haven't had a chance to speak with your trainer, you appear more than ready for your Realization Trial."

I hesitated. "I feel prepared."

It was my standard answer. Look confident. Sound it, too. But it wasn't an honest answer. *Prepared for what?*

Com turned his shoulders slightly, sensing tension ripple around me. "What is your question, cadet?"

No hiding it now. It was nearly impossible to hide any thought from a guy like that. *So how'd he miss those chilly images?*

"I would be able to answer your question with greater confidence," I said, "if I knew what the Realization Trial was about. Pon hasn't given me any objectives. I don't know if I'm swimming across an ocean or jumping out of a spaceship. Tell me what exactly I'm training to do and I believe I can answer you more truthfully."

Com laughed heartily, and the commander smiled. The two assassins had yet to blink. "Yes," Com said, "the Realization Trial is frustrating. Let's just say Pon will have you ready for whatever comes your way, yes?"

I nodded, frustration clenching inside me.

"Another question?" he said.

I was doing a horrible job of controlling my thoughts. I minced them quietly, considering if I was pushing too much. My frustration was too visible. He would only tolerate it so long. *Enough is enough, control your mind, cadet.* But these were my thoughts and, to be honest,

I already knew the answers. In fact, the question was ludicrous. I didn't want to say it out loud, so I just allowed the thoughts to crystallize for him to see my doubts.

[Why are we training so hard? We haven't seen or heard of a duplicate in a year. They've been conquered. Shouldn't we be doing something besides preparing for a nonexistent war?]

Like I said, I already knew the answers. Intelligence suggested that duplicates would have a backup plan, that they would blend into the population until they were ready to strike. After all, they were undetectable. One could be standing right in front of you and you wouldn't know the difference, even if you cut its head off. *It's the predator you don't see that you should worry about.*

Thank you, Pon.

Com saw my question. He also saw the answer in my mind. There was no reason, but instead he said, "Keep your enemies closer than your allies, cadet. That way you always know what they're doing."

"Yes, sir."

He stared a bit longer, judging my stance, my psychic arrangement, my physical conditioning. No need for conversation when you could look directly at one's soul. It cut out all the words and personal agenda.

"I am anticipating record attendance at your Realization Trial." He leaned closer. His breath puffed in my eyes. "I will be present along with every commander in the Paladin Nation."

"I look forward to it."

"I have commended your commander for bringing a prodigy such as you to the great Paladin Nation. It is efforts like his that will make this world a better place." A subtle tension vibrated in the air like electrical currents. He was hiding something. Perhaps it was bitterness or contempt. After all, he wasn't accustomed to travelling outside his facility to see star pupils. They came to him, not the commander. This was a first.

But the energy around us felt tight, almost menacing. I did not adjust my stance, did not want to appear aggressive or tip them off, but instead took notice of the space between us, estimating the range of motion and possible responses to an attack.

"I would argue that you could not find a better commander," I said.

"High praise, indeed." Half-smile for me. Half-smile for the commander. "Very well, then. I will not take up more of your time. I understand you have been given leave for the evening and I sense you're anxious." He nodded and said in a lower tone, "We expect great things from you, cadet."

"Yes, sir."

My heels were still on the edge; I shifted my balance to the front of my feet.

Com started for the exit, the commander beside him. The escorts turned, their motions fluid. The one on the left, his eyes were down, but they cheated a glance back at me. Their momentum kept them turning, their arms falling toward their belts and in tandem they unleashed their evolvers. They spun on their inside heels, pushing their weapon hands at me. Bluish spikes shot forth and space crackled as they sliced time.

But I was ready. I gripped the metaphorical time spark I felt in my belly and stopped time along with them, leaving Com and the commander standing still in normal time. I ignited the evolvers around my hands and deftly parried the tips of their blunt spikes that would knock the wind out of me for a week. Fortunately, they did not counterattack. I was at a woeful disadvantage with my back to the ledge. They retracted their weapons and stood back at attention.

We returned to normal time, where Com and the commander took another step and turned. I deactivated the weapons and placed them on my belt.

"Well done, Commander," Com said. *Half-smile.* "Yes."

The assassins followed them through the exit.

I took a minute to allow my heartbeat to return to normal before doing the same.

4

———————

NORMAL NIGHT Out

THE SERVYS WATCHED me idle the black sedan across the garage and through the illusion of a solid wall into the outside world.

The sun was falling below the trees on the far side of the boulder-strewn field. Behind me, the Garrison's rusty cliffs soared hundreds of feet like a sentinel watching over the world. I stopped the car and let the remains of daylight fall on my face. The breeze rushed through the open windows with scents of bending grass and fallen leaves.

The wheels thumped on the underside of the chassis, folding into the wheel wells, and the antigravity boosters whined into action, keeping the car afloat. The car bobbed slightly off the ground. I twisted the steering wheel, then stomped the accelerator.

The car shot forward and the force threw my head into the seat. The rocky terrain raced under the car. I tapped the stereo and selected Bongo Monday's latest hit, "Parade on Me." The bass thumped in my chest. The Garrison cliffs receded in the rearview screen.

"To review public policy," the car's feminine voice said, "there is no use of antigravity boosters off the Garrison's premises. There is no—"

I turned the music up until my eardrums throbbed and turned the wheel until the car tilted on its side, carving the air in a deep right turn. Lookits, the small silver balls used worldwide for surveillance, tried to keep up, their eyelights watching, reporting back to the Garrison. I yanked the car left and soared to the other side. I'd flown these cars hundreds of times in the simulated training rooms, but there was nothing like the real thing. Besides, simulations didn't have music systems.

I reached the end of the field and slowed onto a barren road that entered the dense forest. I tapped the music down.

"To repeat," the car said, "you will drive responsibly while in public. Obey all laws. Do not engage any automobile functions that are not available to the public. You are due back by sunrise. It is recommended that you get back to your house by two a.m. at the very latest."

"Yessss, ma'am."

A large wormhole bubble warped the space at the end of the road, swirling with blue colors. The wheels touched on the ground and the road bounced below. The first time through a wormhole was like walking through Niagara Falls. Now it was more like getting steamrolled. Still not pleasant.

I came out the other side thousands of miles away from the Garrison. The exit was on a deserted road in the country. Dusky light filtered through the South Carolina oaks, where the air was humid and the rules changed.

Be normal.

CHUTE AND I never lost touch when training started. I went home a lot in the beginning. When I couldn't go home, we met in virtualmode. And when that didn't work, we talked on the nojakk, sometimes until the sun came up.

But then training got for real and those opportunities got scarce. After a while, I barely had time to sleep. At first, days would go by before I could nojakk her. Then weeks. Now it had been months. It was my fault, really. I was too exhausted to return her calls. If I was awake, I was training. I trained so much that I dreamed I was training. I couldn't escape it.

Sometimes, I wasn't so sure if we'd called it quits. The whole long-distance relationship thing was hard enough for two normal people. She had to be having the same thoughts. *Is this worth it? Are we just wasting time?*

I was nervous to see her. Nervous that spark in her eyes would be gone when she saw me. Or maybe I was nervous of what she saw when she looked at me. Sometimes, I didn't feel all that human. I was an outsider. I didn't want her to see me like that. I didn't want to be on the outside while she was inside.

I'm going to puke.

COOPER RIVER BRIDGE was gridlocked and the game had already started. All the major sports were taking a backseat to tagghet. Paladin-sponsored manufacturers rolled out the flying jetter discs to anyone who wanted one. People were learning thought-projection skills at unheard of rates. Virtualmode Internet accounts reached new levels every day. The technology wave was turning into a tsunami. Clearly, the Charleston roads weren't prepared for the madness of a semiprofessional tagghet team.

Chute called while I looked for every possible route around the bridge. She promised to save me a seat. *I can't wait to see you,* she said. That was a good start, but then traffic completely stopped and that took care of the good feelings. Now I was about to rip the steering wheel out of the dashboard.

I considered leaving the car in autopilot and abandoning it, but unattended autopilot was against the law. The car would rat me out. They'd call my ass back across the world if I tried.

There was nothing to do but watch the ships pass and smell the low tide. The car slogged along and I counted my breath. In and out. I settled into the present moment and the tension inside me, recognizing all the expectations attached to it. They were stupid thoughts like: Would she really be happy to see me?

That was pretty much it.

"Left turn in one hundred yards," the car finally said.

I came off the bridge and took the shoulder to catch my turn. I hit the back roads, hugging corners between abandoned warehouses.

"Obey the speed limit," the car said.

"I've been driving two miles per hour for the last hour! This will average out!"

The shortcut didn't last long. The stadium was still four blocks away when I hit traffic again. I wasn't waiting this one out. I yanked the car to the side of the road and parked in front of a row of broken houses. I sprinted down the sidewalk and turned the corner, and there, two blocks straight ahead, was Blackbaud Stadium.

I hardly recognized it. The last time I was at Blackbaud was for a soccer game just two years earlier. They'd added on, since. It was twice as tall. I couldn't see past the imposing wall at the main entrance, but could hear the crowd roaring inside. Lightners floated high above the stadium, illuminating the field and surrounding area.

The parking lot was stuffed. People were hanging around grills and tailgates, raising their drinks when I passed. A red discus tag whizzed over my head, hovering to the other end of the lot, where a kid ran it down and caught it with the curved end of a long stick. He slung it back a few hundred yards to someone on the other side. A bumper sticker read *Just like lacrosse. Only better.*

I stopped outside the main entrance. The line was out to the curb. My nojakk cheek vibrated. Chute's voice bubbled inside my head.

"Where are you?"

I told her where and what I was looking at: a long, unmoving line. The crowd erupted inside the stadium.

"Well, just hurry up!"

A guy pushed out of the line, throwing his tickets over his head like confetti. A three-dimensional hologram glittered on the stub, a picture of a storm flashing over the ocean. The seats were good ones, center pitch, third row. A kid in front of me sucked Coke from a straw, wearing a plastic tagghet helmet with a retractable yellow-tinted visor. The Charleston Squall logo flashed on the sides. He held the cup with both hands, staring at me.

"What's going on?" I asked the kid.

He yanked his dad's sleeve. His father continued shouting obscenities through his hands. The kid yanked again. The father finally looked down. The kid pointed at me.

"They oversold the goddamn game," the father said.

"But you got tickets."

"There's a bunch of counterfeit tickets floating around. The fire marshal closed the gates. Guess who got screwed?"

"But they're your seats, just have them check the stubs."

"What the hell you think I'm trying to do here, kid?"

He turned back to shouting. People started throwing things. Soda cans bounced off the wall over the gates. Not long after that, the metal gates clanged shut. More trash went flying. A cold sensation drained down my neck, followed by garbled sounds, voices that didn't make sense. It quickly turned into a brain-freeze. Suddenly, I was cold again.

Haagloppllls-sssaaaa-sssss-HHHEESGAWTTA!

"YOU ALL RIGHT?" The little kid slurped his drink.

I was on my knee, head cradled in my hands. The sensation went from cold to hot. And I couldn't remember stepping back and getting on one knee.

Why is this happening?

"You want a drink?" the kid asked.

"How about an ice cube?"

The kid popped the lid off and fished out a handful.

"Thanks," I said. My hands were shaking.

The crowd dispersed, but only to the parking lot, where they threw more trash at the gates. Security pushed them farther out. Sweeper mechs hovered out of holes in the stadium walls like mechanical mice, sucking debris into their snouts.

"*Where are you?*" Chute's voice chimed on my nojakk.

I got far away from the entrance and explained the deal.

"*I'm coming out.*"

"You should stay," I said halfheartedly. "You don't need to miss the game."

"*We'll be out in a few minutes.*"

She was coming out. Streeter, too. They would miss the game for me. That was what I wanted to hear.

I WENT over to the grassy park area to the right of the main entrance and sat at one of the picnic tables, massaging the cold sensation that lingered in my neck. The cold fits were getting worse, and now there were voices talking through a watery veil. It wasn't like I was picking up thoughts from bystanders, it was more like energy swelling up inside me. Something wanted out.

Pon can't know about this.

Unexplained experiences weren't good. It meant instability. The Paladin Nation did not look kindly on the unpredictable and unreliable. I already had Pon breathing up my ass, I didn't need to tell him I was broken. It had to be the tension. The night off would help. Seeing Chute, too.

A cup rattled. The kid was standing next to me, holding out the cup of ice. I took it. *Thanks.*

His father called him over. The kid stood there, staring at me. I motioned to his father standing out on the curb. "You better go."

The kid ran and took his father's hand, looking back as they headed out to the parking lot. He waved and staggered along, trying to keep up with his father's long steps, trying to see what was behind him. The world was so big and fast at that age, it was hard to see everything. My father always walked fast, too.

I sucked on the ice. Didn't care how grubby that kid's hands were or how many boogers he had caked under his fingernails; the cold felt good. I tapped out the last cube stuck to the bottom, crumpled the empty cup and tossed it to a passing sweeper. The blinds were drawn on the ticket windows.

I was about to tap my cheek to nojakk Chute when a gate opened and a group of kids stumbled out. One had a red ponytail bouncing on her shoulders. *Chute.* The other four were guys and one of them had his arm across her shoulders. It wasn't Streeter.

My stomach didn't exactly flip with excitement. It hardened like a fist.

5

___

I REMEMBERED those guys from school, a bunch of virtualmode addicts. They were still ugly, but now they sported tagghet jerseys and strutted through the gates like big shit. Jenson had a huge nose, Perry had no chin, and Lee's eyes were too close. The fourth one was Sheldon. He had blond hair. He was the one with his arm over Chute's shoulders.

They bookended Chute—two on each side—and walked close to her. She held a game program and they pretended to be interested in what she was pointing at, but they were slobbering wolves pretending to be sheep. I didn't need to see their thoughts, I could feel their hunger.

My lip was twitching.

Chute ran for me when she saw me. I held out my arms and caught her leaping, spinning her round and round. I buried my face on her neck, inhaled her fragrance. Her energy tingled through my senses.

Her hair was longer. *Were her boobs bigger?*

"Oh, it's so good to see you," she said. "It feels like forever."

The tension in my chest melted.

She squeezed my shoulders. "You're like a machine. What're they feeding you at that place?"

"The same as you, I guess. Look at those guns."

She pulled her short sleeve back and flexed her chiseled biceps. We had a laugh and I was lost staring at her, like I was drinking through my eyes. I'd never forget what she looked like, but time tends to erode the details. It was the brightness of her smile and the wrinkles at the corners of her eyes I'd forgotten.

She introduced her teammates. It had only been a year, but everyone was forgetting me.

"This is Shelly."

"Shelly?"

He uncrossed his skinny arms. "Sheldon."

We shook hands like arm wrestlers, squeezing a little too tight. A little too long. "What kind of name is Socket? You related to Craftsman?"

The others snorted and sort of hid their smarmy grins.

"Shelly!" Chute said, shoving him.

"What? That was funny, come on. You ever heard of anyone named Socket?"

"He's my best friend, so be nice," Chute interrupted before blondie had a chance to say something else. Or maybe he did say something and I didn't hear it. I was still reeling. *Friend?*

We were just friends? And who the hell is Shelly? My mouth hung open and twitched. I hated giving away emotions.

"Where's Streeter?" I asked.

"He's busy, couldn't make it tonight."

"Busy? I get one night off and he's *busy*?"

"You need to call him."

"I will." I reached for my cheek. "I'll call him right now."

"Hey, man. If you got somewhere to go," Shelly said, "we can take Chute off your hands. We got some tagghet business to talk about anyway, so you go call your *little* friend and we got this."

Little friend. That was a crack on Streeter's height. He wanted me to know he and Chute were tight, that they were hanging out and talking when Streeter and I weren't around. He wanted me to think they might even be doing things.

"No," I said. "It's good, I got it."

I tapped my cheek and activated the nojakk, mumbling Streeter's name. The call ticked along, trying to connect. Meanwhile, Shelly put a piece of gum in his mouth and stared at me like he was some badass. Christ, tagghet was making him delusional. The other morons were busy with Chute and her program, but Shelly was itching for trouble. Why couldn't he just play nice? Was he trying to be big dick in charge and I was on his turf?

I could play nice if they didn't come off like possessive jocks. And they weren't even jocks, they were goddamn computer dorks wearing uniforms. The only reason they tagged was because jetters required thought-projection and virtualmoders were prime candidates. Most of them had horrible coordination.

He dropped the wrapper on the ground. "You ever tag?"

"Huh?"

"Tag. You know, *tagghet.* The game we were watching until you couldn't get a ticket."

"Uh, yeah." My call went to Streeter's voicemail. I didn't leave a message. I considered calling again.

"So where do you go to school?"

"Uh, nowhere. I'm homeschooled."

"Homeschooled? You got a homeschool team, is that it? What do you call yourselves, the Homeschool Hippies?" He hit Lee in the chest and the three of them laughed on command. "Homeschool Hippos?"

He smacked the shit out of that gum while he laughed with his mouth wide open. Chute scolded him for being an asshole. But he had the other three rolling.

"You're lucky you don't play us," he said, catching his breath. "I'd beat your ass so wicked your goddamn hair would turn white."

They let loose this time, half-turning, falling over each other.

There was no stopping him, laughing right in my face. He was taking me out of the picture. Chute drilled him in the shoulder this time. Called him a jerk-off.

"Oh, come on, now that was funny." He regained his balance. "He's already got white hair, get it? I'm so good that his hair is already white. Before I even play him, his hair is white. Get it? That shit's funny. Come on now."

"What position you play?" I asked.

"Second lance." He shadowboxed at me and shuffled his feet, throwing an awkward right hook. "The best you'll ever see."

"Lancer, huh?" I picked up the gum wrapper. "You must be quick."

"Dude, I'll make you dizzy."

I was still nodding thoughtfully. He juked around his boys, play-faking moves. When he was done pretend-scoring, he held his hands up like a heavyweight and bounced on his toes.

I folded the wrapper and held it between two fingers. "You dropped this."

He smiled at his boys and swiped at the wrapper without looking but came up empty. He swatted again and missed. I'd barely moved my fingers and he'd whiffed twice.

He stopped torturing the innocent stick of gum and finally looked at me. I turned my hand over, palm up, and the balled-up wrapper rolled into my hand.

"I learned that in homeschool."

He pecked at the silver ball to catch me off guard, but I bumped the wrapper off his wrist and caught it low with my other hand. He swung with his left, just trying to knock it away, and I batted the wrapper back to my right. Now he was swinging wild while the wrapper went back and forth between his hands. His cheeks were flush, but he was chasing the bouncing ball like it was a phantom housefly.

Finally, I popped it high above our heads. He watched it come down, but before he could grab it, I flicked it like a pebble shot out of a slingshot; hit him right between the eyes. His head snapped back in surprise.

It took a second for him to get his wits back. A red dot was glowing between his eyebrows. I had my empty hands up and parted my lips, the silver ball between my teeth.

Shelly tried to smile, but I'd crossed that friendly line. His boys weren't smiling, either. He thought about taking it to another level, but he couldn't fight. He wished he could fight, but he was over his head. All bark, no bite.

Instead of taking a swing, he wrapped his arms around Chute and interlocked his fingers over her stomach, pulling her against him tight. Smiling, sort of. "Let's get out of here, guys."

He thought he had the upper hand, that teammates meant more than friendship, that Chute would choose them over me and that was the best way to strike back, but Chute was about a half second from planting an elbow in his left ear. He crossed her line.

I should've let her do it, but when he touched her like that, I didn't respond. I reacted.

I reached my mind around him like a net and dragged through him like fingernails. Pon had put the brain-freeze on me a hundred times. It was the quickest way to confuse an opponent.

Shelly turned pale and wobbled backwards. She helped him along with a stiff shove. Shelly's knees gave out and his boys caught him before he face-planted in the grass.

Chute stomped off, cursing at all of us. Me included. Shelly might've been a jerk-off, but I was a bully. She knew I did something. I was quickly after her. Shelly, he was drooling.

Maybe she was right.

6

———

A Slice of Time

I was braced for a nojakk call from the Garrison to return for an unauthorized mind read, but I didn't read his thoughts. It was a bare minimum movement of the mind that could be considered an assessment of a situation, nothing they'd censure me for doing.

"I'm sorry, Chute. I just kind of, you know, lost my mind when he—"

"They don't usually act like that."

Maybe she's not mad at me. "They're jealous, that's all."

"They're just friends. They don't have anything to be jealous about."

I sort of half-laughed, half-coughed, and looked away with a loud *eh-hem.*

"What?" she asked.

"Have you seen yourself lately?"

"What's that supposed to mean?"

"I just mean, duh, they're guys."

"And I'm a girl, so what? That doesn't mean we can't be friends."

"No. But they're *guys*. They don't know how to be friends with a girl, especially one that looks like you. Unless they're gay. Are they gay? Because, you know, I was getting a vibe from Lee and I wasn't sure—"

"Listen, we're just *friends*."

Friends. Okay. But a friend could mean anything. Could be someone you call to get something off your chest. Someone that shared notes in class or loaned you money. Could be a friend with benefits. I started to ask the question, to get a little clarification, but I didn't. I had to stop reacting. Besides, the night would go up in flames if I asked something like that. Call it a hunch. I wasn't sure I wanted the answer to that, anyway.

We waited for traffic before running across the street. My car was another four blocks up, all alone beneath a streetlight. We walked in step, the old houses crowded against the sidewalk. Even shared a laugh. After a couple of blocks, she reached over and hooked her finger around mine, and just like that it felt like I'd left just yesterday. Our hands were sweaty, but I wasn't letting go. And Chute was still squeezing.

"Do you want to go downtown?" I asked.

"It's late."

"We can sit at the market café and make fun of tourists, what do you say? Just like old times."

She had a curfew, but a quick call would push it back, especially when her older sister knew she was with me. She tapped her cheek and talked with her dad. It took a little conversation, but when she tapped off, she turned and smiled. "I've got until midnight."

"Who says I'm taking you home?"

She socked me in the arm. Not hard, but directly on the triceps wound. It startled me, felt like she put a blowtorch on my arm. The pain shot across my back and through my other arm. I had to put my hands on my knees for a breather.

"Oh, are you all right?" She bent over, rubbing my back. "I'm so sorry. I didn't realize training had turned you into such a wuss."

"Oh, you're going to get it."

She attempted to outrun me. I caught her four houses down, hoisted her on my hip and carried her like luggage. She laughed and screamed. There was no one around to hear her fake cries for help.

"Oh, you've got such big Paladin muscles," she said, giggling. "Are you taking me to headquarters?"

"Yeah, I am. Then it's right to the dungeon for some old-fashioned torture."

"I'm calling the police!"

"They won't get here in time, but what I'm about to do to you could be considered a crime. My car's right up there."

"I thought maybe you parked in Myrtle Beach. You should've picked me up at the stadium."

"And leave you with Shelly?" I set her down. "Not without Streeter."

She didn't laugh so much at that. It felt like something just happened between us. She was quiet, then said, "When's the last time you talked to him?"

"Last time I saw Streeter? It was like three and a half months ago. Actually, I didn't see him, we met in virtualmode. He took me to this new world he's been working on—"

"I think he's in trouble." She looked at the sidewalk, following the cracks with her eyes. "He's been avoiding me. I call him all the time and he never answers. He's hardly at school anymore. I'm a little worried." She looked up. "You know, that's not like him."

Two people came out the front door a few houses ahead. I followed behind Chute to let them pass and tried to think of anything Streeter might've said or done that seemed out of character. He'd said something about a statewide award he won for codebreaking. What if he went codebreaking somewhere he shouldn't have, like national security? Or worse, a Paladin database? They don't have a sense of humor about that shit.

The two men approached. They weren't well dressed, but they had a bunch of gold chains and bathed in cologne. I accidentally bumped the stocky one.

"I'm sorry about that," I said, over my shoulder. "Chute, did Streeter say anything about—"

Warning.

The men were turning.

No vehicles on the road. Twelve houses have lights on, only nine have a view of us. No visible residents.

Their muscles tightened. I smelled adrenaline surging through them.

Two men. One short, stocky, visible scars. The other is muscular with tattoos. Both twenty years of age. Cologne masking smell of perspiration.

I shifted my weight.

Chute is 4.2 feet away. The curb is 3.5 feet. Sidewalk uneven from a live oak growing 5.1 feet behind me. House is 2.8 feet to the right.

The stocky one was driving his fist at the back of my head. He was fully committed to the swing. I easily moved out of the way and rammed my finger and thumb under his chin, lifting him onto his toes. The jolt to his jugular lit him up. His eyes rolled and, before he became dead weight, I tossed him at the other guy.

I grabbed Chute's arm and started around the live oak. The car was only a half block away. If the taller one gave chase, I'd knock him out, too.

"SOCKET!" Chute screamed. "HE'S GOT A—"

Flash.

The night lit up.

There was no choice.

I triggered a timeslice.

My metabolism went through warp speed, dumping enzymes and adrenaline into my system. Synapses twittered at light speed and I saw, thought and moved at a velocity unknown to ordinary humans. For me, time stopped.

The 9mm bullet was out of the barrel, suspended in space. I shook my head. *The night is over.*

Why would they do it? Was it money? Is that what they wanted? If they'd asked, I would've given them everything just to keep this from happening. But now this? The Garrison wouldn't understand. There would be no forgiveness. I should've assessed the environment, known I was putting us at risk in this neighborhood at night. There was no excuse. *Battles are won or lost before they begin.*

Chute's mouth was open, halfway through warning me that he had a gun. I brushed the hair from her face and touched her freckled cheek. My only night and I blew it. When would be the next? *Never.*

I held her hand and gently moved her out of harm's way. My steps echoed in the silent slice of time. No insects. No wind. Just dead silence. The glittering streetlight reflected off the bullet's metal casing. I slapped it into the road; it tinkled down the storm sewer.

I took the gun from his hands, careful not to touch the flaming barrel, and placed it on the sidewalk where the police would find it. The bruised spots behind his ears were fresh. I pulled the scumbag down and looked into his dark eyes. The pupils were abnormally dilated, the beginning stages of gear addiction. Gear junkies like him forced high levels of endorphins from their bodies with emotional gear manipulators. It was a natural high, but there was nothing natural about it. They turned their bodies into poppy fields, producing their own narcotics.

His breath stank and slimy pockets of spit stuck in the corners of his mouth. Just touching him made the back of my throat tight. I held my breath, penetrating his mind. His foul energy clung to him like smoke. His mind was corrupt like a scratched hard drive, the nervous system twitching beyond his control. His thoughts intermingled with delusions and childhood memories and sour thoughts of crimes he'd committed, some very recent. He was human, but seemed more like a duplication of a human. A copy. A program that followed the orders of his addictions and warped egotism. I was tempted to look inside him with a direct touch just to see how similar he was to a duplicate, but that would be too dangerous, could suck the life out of him. Even if he deserved it.

I let go of time, feeling my body tingle back to the ordinary march of the world. Distant cars honked.

"An unauthorized expression of abilities has been recorded," a voice called on my nojakk. *"Return to the Garrison immediately."*

His eyes darted back and forth. His senses tried to reconnect, unsure if he was dreaming or just high. Then he lost it, slapping at me like a kid trying to escape his father's clutches. I squeezed his mind, overloading his consciousness, and his body surrendered, falling weightless. I laid him on the sidewalk next to his partner and folded their arms over their stomachs. I made a call, giving my coordinates. The police would be here soon.

"What happened?" Chute said.

I took her down the sidewalk, but couldn't get her to look away. I held her close. Her breathing was quick and shallow. She was trying to assimilate the impossible. There was a gun. A bullet. And then what?

Chute knew what I was. She knew what I could do. Still, her mind was ordinary. Those were the sort of things that happened in movies. I hated that she was trembling.

A black car pulled up to the curb. It was from the Garrison, slicing time the moment I broke the rules and coming for us. The driver got out and opened the back door. I helped Chute inside. She was still looking at the bodies, wondering if they were dead. She looked back to me, struggling.

"Where am I going? Are you in trouble? Are they..." She looked at the gun. "Are you hurt?"

"I'm fine. And so are you. The driver will take you home now. You're safe. We're all safe."

She was sorting it out now, grabbing my hand. "You're going back?"

I hooked my finger around hers. I didn't have the words to tell her what I was feeling. She didn't need me to say it, but it would've been nice. The driver fidgeted. Chute's lips quivered, but the words wouldn't form.

The sirens were near.

I watched the black car drive away. Everything I wanted was in the backseat.

I walked down the middle of the road. Blue lights turned the corner a few blocks back and the sirens wailed. People parted the curtains and looked out their windows, but no one came outside. No one would remember seeing black cars. No one would remember seeing the boy with white hair drive away.

7

———

Pets

"REPORT TO THE DEBRIEFING ROOM," was the message I got when I arrived at the Garrison.

I went to the Preserve instead. The order repeated on my nojakk and I marched through the heart of the jungle. The order finally stopped. Someone would come get me. Eventually.

A few miles later, I stepped out of the trees onto a wide open stone slab with an ancient, barren tree at the far end. The grimmets' vivid colors squabbled along the limbs. They stared at me approaching, their golden eyes blinking. Their somber mood reflected what they sensed inside me.

They knew me so well.

The slab dropped off like a small cliff into a pond below, where the tree was rooted. I sat on its ledge and stared at the sparkling water. A red grimmet came over, wrapping his long tail around my neck.

"It was a disaster, Rudder," I said. "A freaking disaster."

I lay back. Rudder reclined on my chest and imitated my posture with his hands behind his head. The moon was nearly full, casting the tree's shadow over me, but the sky was beginning to lighten where the sun was close to rising in this part of the world. The universe was so vast that light travelled 2,500 years just to reach the nearest galaxy. There were a billion galaxies beyond that with billions of stars in each one. It was all so limitless.

Why do I feel so trapped?

I had the power to do things normal people wished for. I knew more about the mind than psychological experts, but I was the one wearing a leash.

Steps quietly shuffled up behind me. Spindle's eyelight softly turned the tree trunk red. He waited quietly while I counted stars, following the Big Dipper to Orion's Belt. Was there someone out there staring back, wondering why life was so unfair, too?

"We must report for debriefing, Master Socket," Spindle said softly.

The grimmets stirred, their golden eyes sparkling like the stars beyond. "Do you know why the grimmets are here?" I asked.

"They aid the Paladin Nation."

"I've been here a year and I don't see them aiding the Paladins. They don't go anywhere; they're not involved in training or explorations. So how, exactly, do they *aid* them, Spindle?"

"Grimmets are masters of psychic technology. They aid cadet awakenings. You have seen them do these things, Master Socket..."

I nodded while he read me the information in his database. He was a company man. Rudder walked to my hand and curled up, closing his eyes, gently purring. I held my evolver up, the one that was damaged during the exercise. It only took a series of thoughts and the grimmets somehow read the technological problems inside and told it to repair itself. It warmed in my hand and I replaced it on my belt. It was fixed. I never had to check their work.

"I have a theory," I interrupted Spindle's spiel. "When the Paladin Nation punched a wormhole through the Milky Way, they found a habitable planet on the far side of the galaxy with these intelligent creatures." I held Rudder up by the tail. "And they said, 'Hey, let's take them home and add them to our collection.'"

"But, my data suggests—"

"They brought them *against* their will, Spindle. Dragged them light-years from their home into this manufactured forest carved out of a mountain and said here's your new home, boys and girls. Enjoy. They brought them here to *serve*. Not to aid, but to serve. Against their will." I stood up and punched each word with emphasis. "Now, do you think that's fair, Spindle?"

"I am afraid your hypothesis is incorrect."

"Yeah? Well, where do you get your information?"

"I am kept up to date with all Paladin records. They are current and accurate."

"You get your information from the Paladins. *They* tell you what *they* want you to know. You don't *know*."

Truth was, I didn't know either. I knew what Spindle told me was the standard answer, but I always had a feeling there was another one. The grimmets never told me anything, but I sensed the flock was restless, like they were waiting for something. It was how I felt, too: like something was supposed to happen and we were just waiting until it did.

Only that something never came.

"You ever get the feeling you're a pet, Spindle?" I pondered the sky. "That you're just some specimen in a collection?"

"I do not understand, Master Socket. The grimmets are a valuable asset to the Paladin Nation. As are you."

Valuable asset. My point exactly.

The grimmets were wise. They accepted their imprisonment. Here they were, trapped millions of miles from home, and they still found peace and happiness. They still found comfort on a distant planet in a dead tree. I was too stubborn or stupid to do the same.

"We must report for debriefing," Spindle said.

I placed Rudder in a hole in the trunk. I could see his glowing eyes watch us as we entered the trees.

8

———

The Dance of Colors

Paladins took notes on my side of the story. I opened my mind to show them the event recorded through my senses, as I experienced it. I did these things because I was a good soldier. I didn't like it, but I put those feelings aside. *Good boy.*

After that, I went back to training. I went back to forgetting what happened with Chute, ignoring how I felt, and I completed my assignments and missions. Pon was busy with Paladin business and didn't have a chance to meet with me, to pick my analysis of training apart. He relayed commands through Spindle. And I completed them.

In my spare time, what little there was, I went to the moldable training rooms and built isolated environments to help forget about home. Sometimes it was a desert, a tundra or other habitat of equal desolation.

Pon returned weeks later.

I WAS SITTING on top of Mount Everest. Snow was piled over my lap like a winter quilt, but the seat carved out of ice was otherwise comfortable. Clouds were strewn below like a cotton bedspread. The air was crisp, rustling my hair. I could not feel the temperature that should've been peeling the skin from my face. It was a balmy breeze, despite the altitude and the deadly ice storm approaching on the horizon.

Ten feet in front of me, a doorway opened in space. Spindle walked up the mountainside, buried up to his waist in snow. A gale-force wind cut between us, pushing him sideways. It whistled in my ears, holding my hair sideways. Spindle's faceplate lit up, but his words were sheared away. He crawled through the snow until he was at my feet. "Perhaps you could return the room to normal, Master Socket?" he shouted.

I flicked my fingers. The clouds and ice dissolved back into an empty white room.

"Are you feeling well?" Spindle asked.

"I don't want to talk about it."

Spindle's face scrambled with colors, but he wasn't able to formulate a response. He looked in one direction, then another. Then, as he often did, returned to the task at hand. "Would you like to consult the evaluation of your training and status now?"

It wasn't a question, really.

"I think it will cheer you up immensely." His face was brighter. "Let me show you the data."

Bright colored bars grew several feet from the floor and rotated, pulsed and spiked. Green, blue, and yellow lines circled the bars like electrical arcs, jumping from one bar to the next. All the colors in the spectrum danced around the room, reflecting in Spindle's faceplate.

"It is my pleasure to translate the analysis, Master Socket." In Spindle's words I was superior, magnificent, and grand. My evaluations were on par with fully realized Paladins. Spindle started with the spiking red bar on his right that represented my raw instincts, citing specific examples in training exercises, even calling up replay videos to point out highlights. Then he moved on to the next bar:

timeslicing ability. The next one was speed and agility, then evolver manipulation, tacking aptitude, combat readiness, and so on and so forth.

They were all *stupendous.*

Spindle didn't seem to notice I didn't give two shits. It struck me I was sitting in a white room, wearing a one-piece battle garb. I plucked it off my skin, rubbed the silky texture between my fingers, and poked it with my thumb, feeling the armorcloth threads stiffen to resist impact. It was white, matching the room. If I walked into the jungle, it would turn green. I swore a long time ago I wouldn't wear something like that, but there I was, listening to an android dance around the room while I sat there in a stupid onesy.

"There is some concern with this bit of data," Spindle announced.

He was behind a translucent pyramidal bar that dwarfed all the others. Its base was as wide as Spindle's shoulders and the tip twinkled near his knees. The surface was pearly, encasing sparkling lights within.

"It appears to be an undefined hidden potential that you have just recently begun to express. However, we do not know what the ability is. It has never been detected before." Spindle stepped through the pyramid. "Are you experiencing anything unusual?"

He was talking about the cold sensation that washed down my neck, and the garbled voices that came with it, the weird visions I had with Com. *Was Pon dead?*

There was something definitely unusual and if my raw instincts were as good as the data suggested, I wasn't telling him. I needed time to sort through it, but I had a feeling I already knew what was happening.

Haagloppllls-sssaaaa-sssss-HHHEESGAWTTA! I heard that nonsense trickle down my neck when I was waiting in line for the tagghet game, when the kid gave me an ice cube. And then I heard it again when Chute said it, just before the gun fired. She was warning me: *Socket! He's got a—Hhheesgawtta... He's got a...*

He's got a gun.

I heard her warn me an hour before it happened. The future was coming to me as a cold, paralyzing sensation, speaking through a thick barrier of time. And I wasn't controlling it.

I looked Spindle square in his eyelight.

"No, nothing unusual."

Spindle waited for me to elaborate, or to perhaps finish my thoughts. I didn't.

He waved his arms and the colored bars, spikes and lines vanished. "Let us move to the training room to prepare for the pre-Trial, shall we?"

"Pre-Trial? That's not scheduled for two weeks."

"There has been a change in the schedule. Pon will soon be temporarily reassigned to assist in Pike's relocation."

"Pike is being relocated? Again?"

"There is evidence he has contacted someone outside his imprisonment. His location is crucial to his isolation. Only trusted Paladins can relocate him."

Pike, the greatest Paladin traitor of all time, had been secretly imprisoned for an entire year, ever since I exposed him. He carried more knowledge about the duplicate population than everyone thought, but it came with a price. Pike was already a superior minder, a Paladin with exceptional psychic skills, including the ability to read thoughts, to see without eyes and to heal minds. Or destroy them.

But his abilities were appearing to grow when they should have been diminishing under the pressure of Paladin minders. In fact, he recently gained control of a minder, drained his personality and will, and turned him into his own personal puppet. The minder turned on his companions, killing one and injuring two more. He was stopped, but was a zombie by then.

"Trainer Pon would like for you to complete the pre-Trial exercise this morning," Spindle said. "This is the second of three pre-Trial exercises required to be completed before the Realization Trial. According to the data, you are ready."

Off to training we went. I was one of the best Paladins of the future. *Why don't I feel like one of them?*

9

———————

RIDDLED

I WAS ALONE in the training room. Fresh air filtered through microscopic pores in the walls, carrying a subtle undercurrent of purification.

It was early in the morning, not that there was a clock. Spindle left at 5:55 a.m., as he did every morning, and let me stand ready in the center of the room, hands behind my back. Pon would arrive precisely five minutes later. He was never late. Never early.

I never knew where he was going to enter the room. It was always a surprise. He could enter anywhere along the walls or through a trapdoor. Once he dropped from the ceiling. Sometimes he strolled into the room. Sometimes he attacked. *Always be ready.*

And he always pointed out something I fucked up. Just once, it'd be cool if he walked in, clapped his hands, and said, "Oh, you've outdone yourself this time, Socket! That's my boy! MY MAIN MAN!"

Instead, he'd drop from the ceiling because he knew secrets. He claimed to know every secret tunnel in the Garrison. Claimed he knew them better than the commander himself. Maybe he dug those tunnels himself because he was *sooo* goddamn important—

"Control your thoughts, cadet." Pon emerged from a solid wall.

I tightened my mind.

He pursed his lips, taking a moment to observe. Then, with his hands behind his back, he paced around me. His footsteps fell like a predator's. I mindfully followed his presence without turning as he walked out of eyeshot. I followed his energy, followed his movements and searched his intentions. He stopped directly behind me and took a balanced stance. His mind reached around, searching for weakness. If I was not vigilant, he would squeeze me unconscious. He'd done it before. That sort of thing was not easy to forget, especially when you piss your pants.

"Tell me, cadet, that I haven't wasted a year training you?"

He probed my mind some more, giving me an opportunity to respond. I wasn't answering that.

He circled around, looking thoughtfully at the ground. The psychic pressure intensified, threatening to push through my barriers and creep inside. If he got in, I would suffer major brain-freeze and, politely put, *go night-night.*

I closed my eyes to steel my mind, whittling my focus down to a tiny point. Weak minds were clay in Pon's hands. He was an artisan who could mold the mind's fabric or squish it between his fingers.

He made a complete circle and stopped in front of me. I remained resolute. Knees flexed, ready to timeslice if he attacked... for the purposes of training, of course.

"You can never go home, cadet. It does not exist for you anymore."

"It was just a visit."

"That life has passed."

"They're friends, like family. I'm not turning my back on them."

"Understand the conflict, cadet. Understand what you wanted your trip to be. You want a girlfriend to hold your hand. You want to do things ordinary people do. You want to be what you once were." He tapped his head. "Those are your thoughts, and therein lies your suffering."

I'll tell you what suffering is. It's training nonstop. Suffering is going a week without sleep. It's breaking bones and gashing skin. It's getting your brain squeezed like a fucking lemon.

"This present moment is vital, cadet. This moment is all there is. The present moment does not care what you think or how you feel, it exists regardless. You exist in it, not separate from it. The present moment is the beginning and the end." He made a circle with his finger and thumb. "Your feelings about it are irrelevant."

What if I don't care?

His eyes were light blue. A psychic storm rushed through his small, sharp pupils and absorbed my thoughts and emotions. I let him see the doubt rumbling inside.

"It feels suffocating, mmm?" he asked. "Emptiness? Uselessness? Is that how you feel?"

"How about uncertainty."

"I see," he said. "And these feelings of apathy suck the life from your focus, mmm?"

"Something like that."

He stood still. Only the room seemed to breathe.

"Cadet, we serve this world, that is our purpose. Our sole directive. Do you think your loneliness is a fair price for that service, mmm? We save the world from itself, not because we *feel* like it. Because it is our duty."

"Not all of them want to be saved."

"They are lost. We are their shepherds."

"And they still don't give a shit."

"We don't ask for gratitude." He lowered his eyebrows. "When the universe cries, cadet, you answer. Do you think life will understand your failure because you don't *feel* like serving?" The words imprinted on my mind, burning like a hot iron. "Growth is difficult, cadet, that is a fact."

He moved very close. His breath streamed through his nostrils. I did not look away. I reached out to him with my mind and pushed back. The room crackled with our energy. My backbone vibrated. His eyes were open and empty. There was never anything to see inside

Pon, but I always looked for a hint of weakness, a clue of motivation. But there was never anyone inside; he was seamless. Pure, like water.

I was rooted to the floor, ready to strike. I was in the room. *In the moment.*

He stepped back. Satisfied. "The Realization Trial is in twenty-two days. If it was today, you would fail."

"I still don't know the objective."

"The objective is simple: You must see."

"I see just fine."

"Says the blind man. The urgency to see clearly, to act directly, is upon you. It is now, cadet. Your preparation is not just physical and mental, it is your entire being. You prepare to be everyone. And to be no one."

"That doesn't make any sense."

"Precisely. The true enemy is within you. But first you must see the enemy. Do you see him, blind man? Do you see the enemy, mmm?"

My body tightened.

Precisely.

Pon stepped backwards. The room transformed with each step. The putty walls turned brown and tan. The floor became sandy and the ceiling an endless blue sky. Boulders grew around me, tall, sharp and dusty. By the time Pon reached where the wall had been, it looked as if the Sonora Desert ran for miles beyond.

"This is a pre-Trial exercise," Pon said. "Defeat your enemy, cadet."

The sun was high above, stinging my cheeks. Spindle looked down from one of the boulders. He was not wearing his plum-colored overcoat. Steam rose from his silver body, the scalding heat bending the air around him.

"That's an image," I said. "That's not actually Spindle, right?"

"Do not hesitate to do what life requires. When you know the truth, action is immediate, decisive and complete."

"I can't destroy Spindle, Pon."

A smile touched his lips. "Spindle is not his body."

"But that's not right."

"Do not fear death, cadet. Embrace it." Pon took one last step, vanishing through the invisible wall space. His voice remained. "For in death, there is rebirth."

Spindle's faceplate was blank. His red eyelight darkened. He had no weapons. He didn't need them. He bent at the knees and touched his fingers on the ground, crouching like a tiger. I touched the evolvers at my belt.

Do not let feelings obscure the truth.

See clearly.

See what is, not what you want.

Why does that fucker speak in riddles?

Spindle sprang to the other wall, puncturing the stone with his fingers, gripping it like a cat on a tree. Pebbles trickled down. Pressure was inside my skull. Defeat my friend.

"*It is not your enemy you fight, but your thoughts.*" Pon's voice was in my head. "*That is the training.*"

Dust obscured my vision. Spindle's dark eyelight pierced the cloud. Pressure built within me, culminating in my chest. I clutched my weapons, bracing for impact.

Spindle would have to die.

10

Dead Battery

"You want a drink?" The kid holds his father's hand and sucks on the straw.

They walk across the parking lot, leaving me on the curb. When the kid turns around, his face is blank. It has a black eyelight.

My chest is tight.

The parking lot is gone. The kid and his father, too. I am pinned against a rock, sand grinding into my shoulder. Spindle is over me, his eyelight black. His fingertips are slowly piercing the bubble shield surrounding me, aiming at my chest.

"Where's Chute?" The kid is back, holding his father's hand. They're behind Spindle.

"I don't know," I say. "Um, where am I?"

"You want a drink?"

He points the straw at me.

Spindle hovers over me, pushing his fingers closer. Slowly, slowly they creep toward my heart. *This is a test. It is only a test. Fail and you die.*

The eyelight is dark.

Pressure.

Ice rattles in a cup. The kid and his father are halfway across the desert now. He's sucking on the straw. I hear him as if he's three feet away. *You want a drink?*

I just, ah... where're you going?

Spindle's face flashes, his fingers an inch away. My chest inflates. Something wants out.

The kid tugs on his father's hand and tries to pull him back, reaching the cup toward me. His father looks down. *It'll be all right, son.*

But he wants a drink.

The father turns. But it's not the kid's father holding his hand. It's *my* father. *It'll be all right.*

I reach, but they are too far. *Wait, wait! Don't go. I... I need a drink.*

Black eyelight.

An eruption. Something gets out.

Spindle is crumpled against a boulder, its surface indented with the force of his body. The boulders, sand and sky disappear into the ground. I'm in a white room. Spindle is sprawled on the floor.

Eyelight out.

I SCREAMED.

"You're dreaming, Socket." Mother placed her hand on my arm.

I was in a bed. The room was warm and spacious. The only furniture was the bed I was sitting on and the chair Mother stood by. Several monitors blipped near the bed. A wide window, across the room, covered the entire wall and overlooked green mountains in the distance. The view cast a glow through the dimly lit room.

"Where am I?" I asked.

"You're in the infirmary."

My left arm tingled where skin was scuffed away. There was a fight. Spindle's fingers. Sand. *Was that yesterday?*

"You were in the pre-Trial exercise two days ago," she said. "But you exhausted your energy levels and slipped into a short coma."

"I don't remember timeslicing. How could I exhaust myself?"

"There were some... unexpected reactions."

"What happened?"

"I don't want to say until we get a full analysis. It's nothing to worry about."

"Did I pass?"

She nodded, then took a note tablet and some recording gear off the nightstand and put them in her briefcase.

"Why am I dressed in street clothes?" I asked.

"We're going home."

"Home? I was just... wait." I looked around. "Where's Spindle?"

She finished packing, stood straight and pushed her hair behind her ear. She blew out her breath, as if it was stale and tired. She tried that fake reassuring smile but didn't even have the strength to do that. "He's being attended to."

"Is he all right? I didn't... he's not hurt, is he?"

"He'll be good as new, Socket, but he'll need some maintenance before he's activated again."

He was slumped against the boulder. There was an indention in the stone, as if he'd been shot from a cannon. No eyelight. He had me beat. He was inches from ending the exercise, but somehow I threw him off. That part was blank. But I saw him, motionless. Lifeless.

"Pon made me do it."

"It's part of training. Spindle will be fine, trust me." She stroked my arm reassuringly. "Now, can you swing your legs off the bed? I don't want you to stand just yet, just let your feet touch the floor."

I just woke up and she was rushing me out the door. Why didn't they just wheel me out to the car while I was comatose? *Maybe that's what she was getting ready to do.*

My feet were cold, tingling with pins and needles. The floor hurt. Mother clutched my arm to slow me down, making sure I didn't try to stand. My weight ached in my shins. I was already breathing hard. The room was getting darker.

"Sit there a second." She touched her nojakk cheek. "I need three servys in infirmary 204 with a floater as soon as possible." Then she muttered to herself, "Where the hell are they?"

"He cannot leave the premises." Pon stood against the wall. *Was he there the entire time?*

"I don't need your permission," Mother said.

"He is my cadet. He will stay."

"He's depleted, Pon! You can read the diagnosis yourself. He needs rest."

Pon stood resolute, hands clamped behind his back. "He needs to focus."

"HE NEEDS REST, GODDAMNIT!" Mother slammed the nightstand, knocking a cup to the floor. "He has barely slept in the past month. He has logged more training hours than any other cadet. He cannot continue at this rate, and I think the result of the last exercise is proof enough!"

"The Realization Trial is too close. He must not lose focus. I insist he remain under my tutelage."

"Your tutelage? You have destroyed more cadets than any trainer in the Paladin Nation. You have wasted so much talent with your relentless antics. You cannot grind them down, Pon. They have to recoup."

They were the same height—Mother was twice as fiery—but Pon could break her with a thought. I eased more weight onto my feet, but even the slightest movement made my head spin.

"Cadets that survive my training are the best the Nation has to offer," Pon said, simply and softly.

"Survive?" Mother said. "The lucky ones survive. Socket isn't going to become one of your *unlucky* ones; he's coming home. Step aside."

Pon considered her demand, then slowly walked over to the window.

Mother tapped her cheek. "Where are my goddamn servys?"

"These circumstances are quite unusual," Pon said. "A cadet's mother making demands of his trainer."

"I'm acting as a responsible member of the Paladin Nation, whether he's my son or not. Set your ego aside and look at the cadet sitting on the bed. He cannot stand. He is of no use to the Nation if he's broken."

"Home will not help him."

"Well, then consider it a vacation."

"I will not tolerate these demands!" Pon shook the walls with a psychic burst. "You will not interfere with my training. *He will remain.*"

The lights dimmed, but it wasn't my clouded perception. Pon sucked the energy from the room. The atmosphere became dense and grainy. I never saw a single loose thought in Pon's mind, but I could tell that he hated dealing with Mother. He didn't like her interfering with his student. And he *never* spoke with his teeth grinding.

[*Always respond, Pon. Never react.*]

He flicked his eyes at me, seeing the thought I projected. Calm settled around him. Deadly, but calm.

Mother shook her head, pushed her short hair behind her ear, and stood in front of me. Pon would have to go through her. But we weren't leaving, either. They stared, daring the other to blink. Mother would eventually wear down under Pon's gaze, but until then, stalemate.

I bowed my head to ease the nausea swirling in my empty stomach. The pins and needles had faded from my feet, but my knees were too weak to hold me. I was going to puke if the room kept circling. I didn't have time for their game of chicken. I needed to feel better, and I didn't care where. Just sitting up was sapping what little strength I had.

The air lightened. A heavy, callused hand squeezed my shoulder. "How are you feeling, son?"

Son. The word chilled inside me, but it was the commander's hand. His eyes were decisive, but gentle. He tousled my hair, then read the monitors, taking his time at each one. He wasn't seeing anything new, but studied them nonetheless.

"Your vitals are good," he said. "You're in fine shape, although I'm sure you feel otherwise."

"I've never felt this weak."

"You were very close to complete depletion."

Depletion was like a dead battery. Emphasis on dead. "I don't remember much."

"Your mind is coping with stress. The memories will come back, although for now it's important that you rest."

"But what happened?"

The commander turned to my mother. She returned his knowing look. Pon had not moved. The secret passed between them, unspoken. The commander rubbed the corners of his mouth. "We're not sure."

Did the icy voice come back? I was careful to hide that thought from them, but one day I would slip. One day, they would see my doubts. My imperfection. I couldn't hide forever.

The commander walked to the window and watched clouds cast shadows over the green mountains. Pon stood soldier-still next to him, eyes ahead.

"Your Realization Trial is near." The commander spoke while gazing out the window. "However, recent events have cast doubt on the exact date. Pike will be relocated in the next few days, and his whereabouts need to remain undisclosed. I will need Pon's service during this time."

Pon did not respond.

"There is also the matter of analyzing this pre-Trial exercise. We need time to fully understand the events before moving ahead with your training. More importantly, I need you to be fully recovered. I would rather sacrifice a week of training than to have you less than one hundred percent. The Realization Trial is too important. While you have so much potential, I have my doubts the Paladin Nation will show leniency if you do not pass. There are still those that doubt your stability."

Shit.

The commander's gaze followed a hawk circling the trees. It

folded its wings and dove out of sight, returning to the sky with something flailing in its talons.

He was not one of those doubters. If he was, I wouldn't be here, count on that. He was a fair man, but not a fool. If he suspected instability, I'd be done. He knew there were Paladins that doubted my father because he altered his own genetic code to give himself Paladin abilities. But his powers failed to stabilize. *And like father, like son.*

The commander faced the room.

"I'm sending you home, Socket. A week in your own house will facilitate your recuperation, after which you can return to the Garrison. There will be no more discussion on this matter."

Mother slung her briefcase over her shoulder, lifting her chin. *Game over.* Three servys floated into the room with a hovering chair. They parked next to my bed. Pon's expression did not change, but I could feel his agitation. *I don't care how you feel, Pon.*

"I expect you back in a week," the commander said. "You mean so much to the Paladin Nation's future, we cannot afford to fail."

The commander paused. I nodded back, not sure if I should thank him.

"Kay, I'd like to see you before you depart," he said. "Pon, if you'll follow me to my office."

The commander exited the room. Pon was rigid. He aimed a glare at Mother. She sensed it and returned one of her own, but it was her cheeks that paled, not his.

I jumped from the bed. The room wobbled. The timeslicing spark ached to be clutched, but was barely able to glitter in my belly. My knees gave way and I collapsed onto the floater chair. The servys' rubbery arms helped me sit up. I panted and could hardly lift my hand.

Pon pursed his lips and blinked slowly. He accepted the decision. And with a slight nod, a warm wave of energy surged through me, vibrating through the pain, easing the aches. I stopped quivering.

Before I could nod back, before I could acknowledge his healing gift, Pon followed the commander. Mother took a moment to compose herself. I floated out of the room on the chair, following the servys. Mother was behind me.

I WAITED IN THE CAR, looking through the clear roof at the parking garage cave and the natural stalactites pointing down like accusing fingers. *You are the chosen.*

Pon was right. I couldn't go home. At least not the home I wanted. There was a house in South Carolina. There was a bed in that house I slept in and a backyard I played in, but that wasn't home anymore. Home didn't exist, not one where I returned from school and lounged in front of the television. A home where I stayed up all night in virtualmode battles and we sat around talking about what we were going to do when we grew up. A time and a place where anything was possible. I was searching for that sort of home.

It didn't exist. Not anymore.

Mother cruised out of the garage into the boulder-strewn field. I rolled my head against the seat to catch the breeze. The air was dry but non-filtered, carrying the scent of nature emerging from the ground. Of growth and decay. *Do not fear death, for it brings rebirth.*

Garrison Mountain was in the rearview mirror, casting a long shadow over the field. It sped into the distance, further into the past. We drove out of the shadow, into the sun. The windows darkened against the glare. I would be back in a week.

The wheels unfolded beneath the car as we approached the tree line, touching the uneven ground, jostling me in the seat. We pulled into the shade of the canopies. The wormhole glittered ahead. We passed through the compressed space and came out the other side, where the air was humid and thick, laced with the fetid aroma of pluff mud and the siren-song of tree frogs. I closed my eyes and let South Carolina in. Mother's instinct was right; I needed to be home.

Or at least a place I could call home, for just a little while.

PART II

For now we see through a glass, darkly.
Bible, 1 Corinthians 13:12

Without pawns, there can be no king.
Pon

11

———————

Crossroads

They weren't far behind.

I squeezed through a narrow tunnel barely wide enough for my hips. It was pitch black, but the shift in air pressure indicated I'd stumbled into a cavern. I flicked open my evolver-wrapped hand, ignited an infrared flame and adjusted my goggles. It was a mineral-rich cavern. Water trickled down the walls, pooling in the center. In infrared, it looked like blood.

I cupped a cold handful of water to my mouth. There were seven openings in the cavern that led in different directions. I needed one to get me to the surface before the enemy found my trail.

My arm was red. That wasn't infrared water; that was blood. I only had about ten minutes before they zeroed in on it. If I moved quickly, I could buy a few more minutes.

I waded into the icy pool and washed my arm, the blood clouding the clear water. The temperature penetrated like death. I came up and pushed my hair away. Six caves were near the ceiling. Most were small. They had a slight glow. Could've been fluorescent algae, or maybe sunlight. The seventh one was behind me. It slanted down-ward and went deeper. It was dark. Water trickled across the sandy floor, finding its way into the bottomless depths of the dark cave. If I wanted to get to the surface, that was a loser.

I closed my eyes, allowed the moment to unfold, and listened to what it had to say. My frigid skin felt shrink-wrapped. I took a deep breath and let it out. The enemy was still far away, but their move-ments echoed distantly, like rodents scratching their way toward food.

Another deep breath.

The air was moving. It wasn't a breeze, just a gentle sway, not enough to even nudge grass seeds on lofty stalks. My breath was shal-low; my chest hardly moved. I followed the slightest motion, letting my awareness drift with it like vapor.

Go deeper.

I had to trust my instincts and follow my assessment. I eased out of the pool and dropped to my knees, felt along the gritty opening, then plunged into the darkness of the cave behind—

"No training!" Mother's voice echoed throughout the network of caves.

I slammed my head on the ceiling, cutting my scalp wide open. Blood streamed down my cheek like sweat, dripping off my chin. The enemy was scrambling toward me.

An hour, wasted.

"Log off, Socket. I need to see you."

I closed my eyes and let my awareness drift out of my sim, through the bodiless in-between, until I felt the flesh and blood of my body. Back in my skin.

I looked around my bedroom while my awareness returned from virtualmode. The posters were curling at the corners, a signpost of life before the Paladins. I couldn't care less about Nine Inch Nails or Dismal anymore. A Jackson Pollock print, the only nonmusical poster, was pinned above the bed. Now that I could still dig. His work was a free-slinging montage of paint splatters, unstructured and just I-don't-give-two-shits what you think. I felt something different every time I looked at it. Some considered Pollock a genius, but he was just as fucked up as the rest of us.

I wiggled my fingers and toes, and ran my tongue over my gums. The transporter imbedded in the back of my neck tingled. It allowed me to transfer my awareness into virtualmode Internet no matter where I was, and in full sensory perception. It just took a little longer reconnecting to skin than usual.

My scalp hurt. There was no cut or blood. It was just a memory. I opened the door. Mother was at the kitchen table, dumping things into her briefcase.

"How'd you know I was training?" I asked, rubbing my head.

"Your imbed was active."

"I had a silencer running. Didn't you think I was sleeping?"

"There's only one reason to run a silencer."

"Maybe I was hooking up with someone. You know, in a social world or something."

She paused to sip her coffee and flicked her eyes in my direction. *Please.*

"You're going back to the Garrison?" I asked.

"There're some urgent meetings."

"When aren't they urgent?"

She grunted, tilting her head in agreement.

"When can I go back?"

"You've only been home two days, Socket. Besides, Pon is still on assignment. There's no point, so just relax."

It felt like two years. The weakness I left the Garrison with was already gone. Well, mostly gone, but I'd been through worse. Sitting around the house wasn't as glamorous as I imagined. The normal world went about their daily lives while I sat around scratching my balls.

I shuffled to the refrigerator and grabbed some orange juice, then fell in a chair at the table. My frizzy hair fell in the cup.

"Why don't you do something today, like get together with Chute and Streeter?" Mom asked.

"Chute's coming over tonight."

"Well, there you go. Get out and enjoy your time off. Go watch one of her games or hang out with Streeter. I'm sure he'd love to have you in the virtualmode lab."

"If I could find him."

She mumbled about forgetting something and rushed to her bedroom. "That reminds me," she called. "He left a message."

Why didn't he just call my nojakk?

"Yes?" Mother said, apparently answering a call. "Yes, I'll be there within a half hour. Make sure the ambassador has a projection pad..." She closed the door.

I finished the juice, spilling some on my shirt next to a jelly stain. "Play messages," I called.

The television square lit on the wall in the adjoining family room. Streeter appeared inside it. Well, it wasn't exactly *him,* it was his animated sim. The details were so good that someone might think it was a real person; that is, if they believed a bloodstained barbarian lived in this world.

"Socket, hey." His bushy mustache shook over his lips. "Just returning your message."

Which one?

"I've been, uh, kind of busy, you know. Things have been weird... not that you'd know." He looked like he wanted to spit. *What's that all about?* "Anyway, I, uh, I'll get back to you later on, you know. Maybe I'll see you at Chute's game tomorrow night."

Message over. No goodbye, no later on, no see you some other time. Just out. He wanted me to see him make that face, see that something was on his mind. *But why the sim?*

"What's wrong?" Mother stood at her bedroom door, fixing her collar.

"Something's up with Streeter."

"What?"

"Don't know. I called him half a dozen times yesterday and then he just sends a message instead of calling back."

"That doesn't sound like him." She checked her face in the mirror next to the front door, then finished her coffee in one gulp. "I'll be back tonight."

"Something going on?"

"Some complications with Pike's relocation." She tipped her cup again, even though it was empty. "There was a slipup in the preliminary move. Pike overwhelmed another minder and nearly escaped."

"You call that a *slipup?* Is he all right?"

"No."

Minders weren't child's play; they were masters of the psychic realm. They could strip a human of all his memories, erase his mind like a hard drive, spin his consciousness around until he vomited. They could will a man's heart to stop with a single thought. They were the most valued of all Paladins. The most trusted. Still, none of them could compare to Pike. In the past, two of them could subdue him. Now he broke them like toys.

"Pon was only supposed to be secondary support," she said. "He's in charge of the move now. I doubt he'll be back to the Garrison until next week, so, you see, there's no point in you coming back. Your trainer's busy."

"When are they going to just kill Pike?"

"That's not Paladin policy."

"How many people have to die to change it? Three minders are dead, you know; and they wouldn't be if we just got rid of him. Three lives for one, the math doesn't work."

She rinsed the cup and placed it upside down in the sink. She stared out the window. "Sometimes it's hard to know the right thing."

"Yeah, well, the right thing is to get rid of his ass. It might stink, but that doesn't make it wrong."

She dried her hands, then pushed my hair off my face and looked at me. She'd been doing that more often lately. Like she knew something. If she did, she didn't let on. Or maybe that was what happiness looked like on her.

"You'll be home for dinner?" I asked.

"I'll be later than that. Why don't you make dinner for Chute?"

"Believe it or not, I was kind of thinking that. But, you know."

"You know what? Don't be wishy-washy, make some food. She's not going to care what it tastes like. I'm leaving the car, so go to the store."

I walked her to the door. A black sedan stopped at the curb. The driver's door opened. There was no one inside, having driven from the Garrison on autopilot. She dropped her briefcase in and waved goodbye.

I WENT to the front porch and propped my feet on the banister. Fragrant tea olives were in early bloom. I noticed things like that now, like the density of humidity, the clarity of the sky, the taste of fresh juice. Since training began, my senses continued to open. New experiences presented themselves everywhere; even the simple things like subtle scents or textures were exciting. It seemed lame to say it like that, but the world was everywhere. I just needed to see.

A school bus squealed around the corner. The passengers stared through the dirty windows like zombies. Some days I wished I could be sitting on a school bus again, mindlessly carted off to school, where I could whittle the day away. At least boredom didn't kill you. But then again, sometimes it felt like it.

Streeter wasn't on the bus. Maybe I didn't see him, or maybe he drove his grandparents' car. I had a feeling it was none of the above.

"Locate Streeter," I said, touching my cheek. My nojakk linked up with Streeter's and calculated his location.

"Streeter is currently at 724 West Market, Charleston, South Carolina."

A house call was in order.

12

GATES **of the Dead**

T**HE WHITE HOUSE** was thirty feet from the road. The shades were drawn. The driveway was empty. Streeter's grandparents never parked in the garage because there wasn't room. It was strictly storage. They never threw anything away and I'd dug through that mess with Streeter a thousand times looking for a plate or lamp his grandmother just knew she'd put in there.

I stepped onto the front porch, past the wicker chairs and potted ficus trees, stopped at the door and listened. Nothing stirred inside. Maybe my nojakk was wrong and he wasn't there, or maybe he was just late for school and missed the bus. Maybe his grandparents took him. *So why am I tiptoeing?* Because the energy around the house was foreboding, like a ghost was in the attic.

I knocked. It echoed inside. Knocked again.

There was a key under the ficus. It had been there since I was five. I could use it, but it would be hard to explain if his grandma came home and, on the chance Streeter wasn't home, I was wandering around inside.

The small surveillance eye, about the size of a marble, was still above the door. The surface swirled. It was still working. Something wasn't right. The house just felt... dark.

I hopped the privacy fence and crept up to the first window. The shade was drawn on Streeter's room. I cupped my hands against the window and peered through a gap below the shade. The desk and dresser were covered with clothes, and the floor wasn't visible under books, papers and Internet gear. Nothing had changed.

The bed was in the corner with a mess of covers. I thought about going around back and looking through the kitchen window, when the bed twitched. A hand was sticking out, fingers twiddling on the mattress. A cable stuck out from under the pillow.

Virtualmoding.

He was on the Internet, virtualmoding in his giant sim. He knew I was at the front door, that surveillance eye would've reported the view to him. In fact, there was another eye somewhere outside his window, watching me watching him.

"Streeter!" I tapped the window. "I need to talk to you, get up!"

His fingers stopped twitching.

"I see you, I know you're in there."

It wasn't enough.

"I'll get the key," I said. "I'll let myself in and drag your ass out of bed."

He still wasn't moving. Maybe the key wasn't there anymore. Slowly, the mound came to life. Streeter sat up.

No way.

He was still short, but thirty pounds lighter. His face was dark. He rubbed his eyes and stretched, pulling the oversized transporters from behind his ears. He sat on the bed, slumped over. Thinking. Maybe I was going to have to get the key after all. But then he stood. He used to be built like a hot air balloon. He'd sprung a leak.

The door was open when I got to the front porch. Streeter was walking away.

"You all right?" I followed him to his bedroom.

"I'm not feeling well."

I touched the lamp on his desk, lighting his room. Dark energy pulsed around him. His breath was shallow, as if it didn't matter whether he stopped breathing altogether.

"What's wrong with you?"

"I got the flu or something?"

"Flu? Dude, you're half gone!"

"Yeah," was all he said. He wouldn't look at me. "I've been puking a lot."

"Have you been to the doctor?"

"It'll pass."

"But you've lost all that weight. Something's not right, you got to get it checked out."

"Maybe I'm on a diet."

"Why didn't you tell me you were sick?" I said. "I haven't seen you in three months—"

"Look, I'm sick!" He bristled with hot energy now. "What d'ya want me to say?"

I pulled the shade and flooded the room with light. His color was all wrong. He blinked at the bright light and sat back down on the bed. I grabbed his face with both hands, forcing him to look directly at me. His pupils were dilated; the rims of the irises were blurry.

"How long have you been virtualmoding?"

"I'm not gear-addicted." He knocked my hands away.

"You didn't answer the question."

"I know what I look like; I'm not addicted!"

"Look at the signs, man! Your eyes are the first to go! You look like a freaking withered-up gearhead."

"Yeah, and what do you know?"

"Face facts! Do you want to feel better or what?"

"Don't pull that Paladin shit on me! I know more about virtualmoding than you'll ever know!"

"What?"

He struggled to stay still. He pulled the shade down and sat at his desk, shaking his leg. He wanted me out of there in the worst way, but knew asking wasn't going to do it. It wouldn't be hard to pick a few thoughts from his mind; they were scattered like fallen leaves. It would be as easy as dragging a net through a school of minnows. My mind reached around him, gently applying pressure. I didn't want to get inside him, just see a loose thought or two.

"Don't pull that bullshit on me!" he said.

"What're you hiding?"

"I got a life, so just stay out! You wouldn't know about it. You and Chute."

"What're you talking about?"

He sat there drumming his fingers on the desk, grinding his teeth, and finally said, "You're not around, Socket, so it doesn't matter. Neither is Chute. It's just me. Just me, bro. So why don't you leave me the fuck alone."

"I'm here to see you, not somewhere halfway around the world, you nut."

"Where you going to be next week?"

His eyes were larger than ever. He was sensitive to thoughts, even though he couldn't control them. That was how he felt me looking inside him. And that was another sign of gear addiction. He needed help.

"You got to stay off virtualmode, man," I said. "It's killing you."

"I'll do what I got to do."

I looked at the box on his dresser. "I'll take your transporters."

"You don't think I have backups?"

"Streeter, this isn't right. I'll bring Chute here, if that's what it takes. She'll make you do it."

"Give me a break, she doesn't have time." He held his belly and burped. "I got to puke now. You know the way out."

He crossed the hall and slammed the door on the bathroom.

He was always vigilant about gear addiction. In fact, he always made sure Chute and I had safeguards on all our gear before we went virtualmode. He checked records to maintain proper hours. In fact, the only way to abuse virtualmode was to disable the safeguards. Virtualmode would shut down if it sensed addictive symptoms. What was he doing? Better yet, *where* was he doing it?

It sounded like a dry heave in the bathroom. How long would he fake that until he thought I was gone? I grabbed the disc-shaped transporters wired to the black box off his dresser. It was cheap-ass gear. Nothing was wired these days, but Streeter could make anything work. This was crap he got down at a gear swap for next to nothing. It was probably easier to disable the safeguards so he could virtualmode endlessly.

I slid the transporters behind my ears, felt them suck against the skin and search for my nervous system. My awareness left my skin sitting on the bed, floating through the bodiless in-between until I landed in a giant sim.

I was ten feet tall in a small white room with no furniture or monitors. Streeter's gear didn't even recognize I wasn't him. The enormous body felt sluggish and powerful. The environment was cartoonish and senseless: no feeling, no smell.

"Take me to the last destination," I called in a deep, gravelly voice.

The walls jiggled, searching the coordinates for the last place Streeter was at. The walls weakened, then crumbled. An imposing metal gate appeared before me. It was thirty feet high with sharp staves on top of the bars, hinged to ivy-covered brick columns. Beyond was solid darkness. The night sky was covered with clouds, but a full moon peeked through an opening, illuminating the weedy path in front of me.

"State your target," a creepy voice said from the other side.

"Where am I?"

"The Gates of Death."

"What's that?"

Pause. "If you need orientation to navigate this world, please enter the room on the right." There was a mausoleum buried in overgrown vines. "Otherwise, state your target."

"Just tell me what this place does."

Another long pause. "Gates of Death is a database of all those deceased. You may visit celebrities, historical figures, family or friends."

Family. "As long as they're dead?"

"State your target."

This wasn't Streeter's style. He was a smash and bash guy. He went to battleworlds, not historical. He didn't look back, he looked forward.

"Take me to my last target."

The gates opened slowly. The dark beyond took form. Colors and shapes emerged from the darkness. Water sloshed in an ocean. Trees sprouted—

Click.

The world disappeared.

I was yanked through the in-between like a fish snagged on a hook and slammed back into my skin. I tumbled off Streeter's bed. My stomach churned. Streeter's dirty socks hung off the ends of his feet near my face. He held the transporters in his hand.

"What were you doing?" he said.

"You can't rip those off like that. My nervous system—"

"*What were you doing?*"

I leaned against his bed, taking a moment to catch my breath. "I saw the gates. Is that what this is all about?"

"You have no right—"

"I'm your friend, Streeter. I'm not trying to take anything from you or... or... listen, you're a goddamn mess, man! You can't keep doing this."

He turned his back on me, facing the corner like he was in time-out.

And then I knew.

"You're looking for your parents."

He twiddled the transporters in his fingers. "This is none of your business."

I didn't budge. Instead, I emitted a soothing energy, filling the room with a calming, loving, embracing essence that permeated his radical aura. The energy settled around him. He started to say something, but the sweetness of the essence felt too good, penetrating his jagged mind. Calming it. Relaxing. Opening.

When his posture released the tension, his shoulders dropped and his fists opened. He fell into the chair at his desk and slumped over, dropping his face in his hands, rubbing his tired eyes.

"I was doing research for history class and stumbled onto the gates," he said. "I talked to Einstein about the atomic bomb and his theory of relativity, pretty standard shit. He didn't tell me anything new, really, but the details were good. I was about to leave and just had a thought. I didn't really think they'd be there..."

He didn't finish. Streeter never talked about his parents, even when we were little. They died when he was five, about the time my dad died, but he said he didn't remember much. Always figured he felt the same way I did about my father, really. It happened a long time ago, so what was the point of bringing up memories? That was then. Now is now.

"That's all?" I said.

Energy spiked off him. "THAT'S ALL?"

"No, I just mean—"

"Imagine your dead fucking dad walking into the room, right now. You think you'd be a little freaked out? You think you'd be like, oh, hey, Pop, how's it hanging? YOU THINK THAT'S HOW IT'D GO?"

"What I mean is the gates is just a game world, it's not real. Those weren't your parents, it was just an image. You're talking to data."

He twisted in the chair and stared a long time. "You think you're better than me, is that it? Or do you just not have feelings anymore? Which is it, Socket? Huh? Are you just a robot programmed to save the world now, is that it?"

He shoved me against the bed.

"I'm no superhero, Socket, I can't control my thoughts and feelings or, or... stop time or any of that horseshit. I'm like everyone else, just trying to get by. So, yeah, it's just a game, I'm sorry. I can't handle my feelings, boo hoo. But I didn't ask you to come in here. I didn't ask you to give a fuck. I GET IT!"

"I'm sorry, I'm sorry... I just thought..."

"You thought it shouldn't matter, seeing my parents? You don't understand, that virtualmode world is as close to being real as this right here." He thumped his chest. "I thought you might get it, but clearly you're not human anymore. It matters to me, superboy. It matters to me."

The front door opened. Bags rattled somewhere in the house.

"You need to leave," Streeter said.

"Hang on a second—"

"Granny?" Streeter called.

His grandma looked into the room. "Are you feeling all right, darling—oh, you have a friend. Good."

"He was just leaving."

"Hi, Granny," I said.

"Hello, darling." She looked confused and held out her frail hand. "What's your name?"

I'd been coming over to the house all my life and she'd forgotten me after a year with the Paladins. I shook her hand gently.

"I'm not feeling good," Streeter said. "Could you take him to the door?"

"Certainly, sweetheart."

He stood in the corner and watched me leave. His grandpa was in the kitchen, putting away the groceries. He waved as I passed. What else do you do to a stranger but wave?

Granny stopped on the porch. "Please come back," she said. "He needs company."

I should've told her to unplug the transporters, but Streeter would find a way to fire them back up. We spent many nights in virtualmode without them knowing. And what was I going to tell her? Your grandson is visiting your dead daughter? Oh, and I think he's gear-addicted.

I should've.

13

———

The Fade

I PULLED the glass dish from the stove. The baked salmon flaked apart with a fork, just like the directions said it would. It seemed like if I was going to screw up dinner, it shouldn't be fish, but the guy at the market recommended it, said all I needed to do was throw some butter and brown sugar on it and bake. Even a dope can't mess that up, he said.

I turned the stove off and slid the dish back in to keep it warm. What was I going to tell Chute about Streeter? I couldn't lie, but she'd want to know. She'd been calling him, even knocking on his door. She just wasn't willing to peek through his window like I was. He was lucky she didn't see him; she would've dragged his ass to the hospital, no mercy.

So, if I told her the truth—how he looked, the thing with his parents—she wasn't going to stay for baked salmon no matter how it tasted.

I'd tell her after dinner.

A CAR DOOR SLAMMED.

I checked the sweet potatoes, making myself look busy. I didn't want to look like I'd been looking out the window for the last forty-five minutes. My heart thumped when she knocked. *Get a hold of yourself, man!*

"Come in!"

I was bent over the stove, pulling the dish out when she came in. Then I stood there like I forgot where I was, staring at her. She didn't need to dress up or do the makeup thing. Just the way she was, right then, it was perfect.

"I came right from practice." Her braids were frayed like she came over on a motorcycle. "I'm sorry, but Coach worked in some new plays."

I was still standing. Still staring.

"I'll go clean up," she said.

"Yeah, yeah," I said. "Use my mother's bathroom. I've got a few things left to do. Um, it's over..."

"There." She pointed. "Yeah, I've been here before."

I ARRANGED each filet on a plate, then spritzed them with lemon. I split two sweet potatoes and hit them with butter and reached for the spinach salad, hitting that with cherry tomatoes, sunflower seeds and parmesan cheese.

"We're expecting a record crowd at the game tomorrow night," she called from the bathroom. "They're saying more people will be there than football. They're talking about two or three *thousand* people showing up. Can you believe it?"

I lit the candles on the table. I called the television on and a fire crackled on the screen.

"I'm getting a little nervous, thinking about it," she said. "The expectations..."

She stepped into the living room. Her face was radiant. Not in the way someone steps out of the shower or returns from the beach, but bubbling with this essence of pure joy, like one of those paintings of patron saints with the halos. I was staring, again.

"You expecting someone special?" she asked.

"Not anymore." I pulled out a chair. "*Madam.*"

She curtsied and danced to the table. "Why thank you, kind sir."

I went back to work on the salad, focusing on cutting cherry tomatoes and onions.

"It smells good," she said. "Who cooked?"

"The chef is in the house, my lady."

"Are the Paladins training you for housework?"

"Cooker, cleaner, and slayer of evildoers." I slid a plate in front of her. "They leave no stone unturned."

She closed her eyes and hovered over it, letting the steam drift against her face. She forked a small piece of salmon in her mouth. "Oh, my." She moaned. "Oooooooh, my."

She dug into the food. Her lips glistened with butter and the fire popped on the wall. I watched her eat half of it then tried some. That market guy was right on the mark. It was freaking awesome. Chute hardly opened her eyes, and when she did, they were brilliant.

The whole scene was like a romance novel. Pon would shit. If he could see me sitting around like some star-crossed, zit-popping teenager, his head would explode.

"Did you see Streeter?" she asked.

"Yeah, I saw him earlier. You know, this morning."

"He's not right."

"Yeah, well, no... he's not well."

"What do you think's wrong?"

I chewed slowly, watching the flames dance on the candles. There were so many ways to answer that question, none of which were lies. Most of which weren't exactly truths, either.

"I didn't get a chance to talk to him all that much," I said. "His granny wanted him to rest. So, you know."

"Maybe we should go over there."

"He's coming to your game tomorrow night," I said quickly. "We're planning on getting together afterwards. The three of us, you know. Just like old times."

Now that, the second part... yeah, that was a lie. I'm pretty sure the first part was, too. Even though Streeter *said* he was going to her game in the message, I knew he was lying, so in a way I was lying. *Just go with it, stop thinking about it.*

Things were just too good. Streeter could wait until the morning, right? What were we going to do if we went over, anyway? It wasn't like he was going to let us in, and his grandma wouldn't know who I was, so nothing was going to change. I just wanted this night, that was all. Not too much to ask.

"He misses you," she said. "He won't tell you that, but I think that's what's going on."

"It's more than that, I think."

"He's just having a hard time since you left and I think some things are coming up. He doesn't feel like he's got anyone."

"Don't we all."

"He's got it worse."

I clutched my fork. "He's got great grandparents, he's one of the smartest guys around, and he's not starving. Is it really all that bad?"

"He's got no one, Socket, that's all I mean. Making friends is hard for him."

"Well, maybe he needs a new skill."

Chute looked at me strangely, not sure what to say. Even I was a little surprised by the tough love I was spewing.

"Look, I'm sorry," I said. "Sometimes I forget what it's like to be normal. I know it's all relative, but we can't save Streeter. Only Streeter can do that."

"We need to be there for him."

"I know, I know," I said. Desperation was creeping through me. "You're right. We'll get with him tomorrow night at the game. Who knows, maybe everything will sort itself out by then."

"You sure he's coming?"

"He said he was." *That's what he said, swear to God.*

She pushed her food around, contemplating. I turned my attention to my own plate, avoiding the temptation to *look* at her thoughts. Soon, she was eating again. Eating until everything was gone.

***

THE EVENING WAS COOL, but humid. The sun was down, but the sky was still lit. Chute hooked her arm through mine and laid her head on my shoulder. I couldn't have scripted it better. We walked down the sidewalk, stepping in time, occasionally tangling our feet and laughing.

An old woman was at her mailbox, sifting through a wad of magazines.

"Hi, Mrs. Higgins," I said.

She looked up from her cache and squinted. "Hello."

Chute looked back. Mrs. Higgins was already on her front steps. "She acted like you were a stranger."

Yeah, the lady I lived next to most of my life. I watched her dog when she was away. She brought cookies over at Christmas and always sent a birthday card with money and a note that read, *Don't spend it all in one place.* And now she just said hello to me, a little nervous about the longhaired teenager walking past her house.

"She doesn't remember me."

"Oh no." Chute squeezed me tight. "She has Alzheimer's?"

"No, she's all right, as far as I know."

"Then what's her problem?"

"It's a Paladin thing," I said. "They call it fading."

"You're turning invisible?"

"Yeah, that's it," I said. "No, it's just that anonymity is important to Paladin service. People forget us easily. We naturally emit energy that loosens memories to fall away from the mind. Now you see me." I waved my hands in front of my face. "Now you forget."

"Why?"

"It makes things less complicated. We can function with less attachment to relationships. At least that's what they say."

"I don't like that."

I didn't want to tell her I didn't mind it. I wasn't big on conversation anyway. Now that people forgot me, it wasn't rude for me to just avoid them.

————

AZALEA PARK WAS DENSELY WOODED with stalwart pines and light-hogging magnolias. Cars were parked in the narrow slots between the trees. We walked through leafy corridors on the mulched paths. Chute slid her hand down my arm, her fingers twining with mine.

We crossed over a footbridge and found a bench at the koi pond. An enormous sculpture of a swan spread its wings in the center among water lilies and cattails. Another couple was tossing bread crumbs on the water and the greedy fish fought for them. We watched them giggle and snuggle. It was sickening, but I was doing the same thing, so I needed to shut up.

Several ducks hopped into the water, swimming after the bread crumbs that landed on the lily pads. They squawked at each other, nipping at each other's wings to get the food first. Everybody wanted a piece. The couple threw the rest of the bag into the water to let the ducks and fish work it out before leaving.

"I'm about to fall asleep." Chute rested her head on my shoulder again.

"It's still daylight."

"It's a school night," she said. "I've got practice in the morning."

"You know, we used to goof on the jocks, and now you're one of them."

I expected her to slug me one, maybe even walk away. I revealed what was on my mind. Maybe I was trying to get rid of some guilt, trying to blame her for Streeter. The way she said it at the table made it sound like his situation was my fault. I was a Paladin; I didn't have a choice to leave him. But Chute didn't *have* to play tagghet. She left because she wanted to.

"I've followed you and Streeter all my life," she said, "did all that virtualmode fighting and camping out when we were little because y'all wanted to, but I never really cared all that much, you know? I just needed something that was mine. Tagghet's mine, it's not yours. It's not Streeter's. It's mine."

She watched the ducks spread out on the water.

"Listen, I didn't plan on playing tagghet, but I'm good at it and I want to share it with both of you. I want you at my games, to cheer me on. It's not the same when you're not there."

I bit my lip. I was having some stupid thoughts that didn't need to become words. Maybe I was jealous she had something besides me. Jealous she *loved* something besides me. I wanted to be the center of her universe, not tagghet or anything else. I wanted to be her everything. *Stupid.* She was no sheep. And that was why I was so into her.

The magic was slipping away from the evening. It was going to end as horribly as the last time. Last time, someone shot at us. This could be worse. Panic clenched my chest.

Chute wandered to an old bubble-gum machine and inserted a coin. When she turned the handle, the ducks raced toward her. She caught the fish food falling out of the dispenser and flung the kernels at the foot of the sculpture. The ducks went after it.

"I know I'm not saving the world," she said. "It's just a stupid game, I know, but it's what I do, Socket. We all can't be heroes."

"I'm no hero."

"Yes, you are." She tossed more food in the water. "You stop time. You do things with thoughts. I'm not even sure how human that is, to be honest. That's a lot for us to live up to. Streeter feels the pressure, too."

"I didn't do that to Streeter. He's got his own life."

She poked at the remaining food in her palm. "Did you forget what it's like to be ordinary?"

Something like that should've hurt like a poke in the eye, but she wasn't saying it like an accusation. She wished, at some level, things were the same as before, I thought. That the world's problems didn't get in the way. It was so easy when we were kids. Dreams were anything we wanted them to be, but now reality was here and it was so complicated. It wasn't always what we wanted it to be.

She gazed in her hand like the answer was in the fish food. I walked over and took it from her and scattered it over the pond. I took her hands. She looked into my eyes with an intensity that could've matched Pon. She grazed her fingertips over my face like it was Braille.

"They won't make me forget you, will they?" she asked.

"That's not possible."

We embraced for an eternal minute while the insects sang. She turned her head. I pressed my lips against hers. They were warm and wet and we melted together. Our energy mingled, open and defenseless. Her vibe was sweet and filling. I squeezed her tighter, closing my eyes and swimming through a swirling tide of emotions.

Pon said I couldn't come home. He was right. This was someplace entirely new.

Chute jumped away and I was left empty-handed, still in mid-kiss. The ducks waddled after her, snapping at her hands.

"They want more!" I said.

"I don't have any!" She scampered backwards and the ducks gave chase. She squealed with delight, yelping each time they snapped. It was the best sound in the world.

"Make them go away!" she shouted.

"Just throw at the water!"

She faked a throw and the ducks went after the imaginary food. We made our escape down the dark path.

The emotions were intoxicating, but each step took us closer to my house and the moment got farther away. The kiss was already a memory; it would stay at the koi pond. It wouldn't last. It wasn't meant to. Maybe that was where Streeter was stuck, coming back to the cold empty present moment when he'd rather be in a world with his parents.

Truth was, reality could suck.

We stopped at her car, holding hands. She bumped her forehead into my chin and I kissed it. No need to go any farther. And then she left.

I stood in the street, watching the taillights turn at the corner. I stayed there, attempting to hold the moment, but it slipped away. There was no choice but to let it pass. I went into the house, wondering when I'd have another moment like that. Reality was already starting to ache. Just another sacrifice a Paladin makes.

Do you think reality cares how you feel?

I DIDN'T SLEEP much that night.

I stared at the Pollock poster, sorting through my thoughts. My emotions were like a boiling cauldron. One second they were sweet and dewy. The next, black smoke.

Did you forget what it's like to be ordinary?

Mother came home after midnight. She cracked my door and I closed my eyes, pretending like I was sleeping. My emotions finally settled. And it was then that I gave way to sleep. It was fast and deep. Restful, until I dreamed.

I dreamed I had fallen through thin ice. I flailed for safety, but the ice kept breaking. I sank into the cold black depths, too heavy to swim. Someone called to me. A voice gurgled through the water. It was far away and distorted.

"Help," it said.

I awoke, startled. Light sliced through the blinds. A chilly sensation was still on my neck.

The voice was mine.

14

———

Old Friend, New Body

Next morning, there were messages from Mother. I'd be returning to the Garrison at the end of the week. There was no time to waste; I went to Streeter's house. I couldn't live with myself if I didn't, not after the half-truths I told Chute.

There was no car in the driveway. I didn't bother knocking, just went around the house. His window shade was up, his bed made and the virtualmode transporters on the dresser. Turns out, he wasn't home. GPS located him on the Interstate, heading for Charleston. Maybe his grandparents opened their eyes and saw him wasting away. There were plenty of good doctors in town, ones that specialized in gear addiction.

I nojakked him and got his voicemail.

"Streeter, hey, it's Socket. Listen, I'm sorry about barging in on you yesterday and snooping around, but you should've seen yourself, man. You needed an intervention in a bad way. My only hope is that you're getting help. Listen, I'm sitting on your front porch right now. I'm going to hang out for a couple hours in case you get home. I'm probably leaving at the end of the week and don't know when I'll be back.

"I want to see you before I go. I'm sorry about the mess you're in. I miss hanging out with you and Chute. I wish it wasn't like this, I really do. If I don't see you today, I hope you can make it to her game tonight. Just ring me when you get there. Maybe afterwards, you and Chute and me can stop for a bite and live some old times. You know, like we used to. Anyways, hope to see you soon, buddy. Take care."

I stayed on the front porch the entire two hours, just like I said I would, occasionally checking the time, but for the most part I watched traffic. When two hours were up, Streeter was still downtown. Seemed like going to a tagghet game that night was not likely. I'd have to come back to his house the next day. This time, I'd bring Chute.

At least Granny would remember her.

THAT AFTERNOON, I got more updates from the Garrison, this time an encrypted message through a secure connection. The message was narrated by a standard animated voice, announcing the planned funeral for one of Pike's victims. The other two victims were undergoing psychic decompression, but they were expected to make full recoveries. The Garrison would be back to standard operation within three days. Just in time for my return.

Pon was in transit, probably still occupied with Pike's secure imprisonment. I didn't expect to hear from him until I was back. For some reason, I wanted to hear his voice again. *I must be losing my mind.*

I was in the kitchen when the imbed planted in my neck began to tingle, spreading around my scalp like electric fingers. I hadn't triggered it to activate. It blurred my vision as it connected with my nervous system. Suddenly, someone was in the room.

Pon faced me, hands locked behind his back. I was seeing him, but he wasn't really there. No one else would see him, though. He was transporting his image directly into my eyes.

Pon looked around, left and right, and smirked: A guttural acknowledgement of my home. *Not a recording.*

He looked back at me. "Good morning, cadet."

I nodded.

"You'll be reporting to the Garrison in three days. I expect you to be fully prepared to continue training. I will not accept any reduction in your physical stamina. You will present a full synopsis and demonstrate a true understanding of your last exercise."

He outlined the physical exercises to be completed before returning and also explained that a virtualmode environment would be uploaded to my link along with a mission statement to be completed, which also had to be analyzed. I wasn't sure if my mom approved, but I wasn't going to ask. Sooner or later, I'd be back in the training room and she wouldn't be around.

"Is Pike secured?" I asked.

"Do not concern yourself with such matters." He paced to the right, stepping over a crumpled shirt. *Is this really a projection?* "I want you to remain focused on your training. Other matters will unfold as needed." He stopped, lifting his chin with a slight nod. "Engage only in the present moment."

The electric fingers released my scalp and my eyes stung as the imbed disconnected. Pon disappeared. I touched the back of my neck. No one said the imbed could do something like that, but then maybe Pon was the only one that knew how.

***

THAT EVENING, I was in the backyard, doing pull-ups on a maple tree, when a car pulled into the driveway. Two doors slammed, but I couldn't see who it was. They went inside the house, through the front door, so I snuck in through the back. It was Mother, all right. She was in the kitchen, talking with someone dressed in a long, black overcoat with the hood pulled up. His long boots were cinched tight over baggy pants. He took a plate from her. His hand was silver.

"Spindle?"

Spindle pushed the hood back and the red eyelight spun on his smooth faceplate. "Master Socket!"

"You're alive!"

"I am, Master Socket! I am alive!"

"But... the last time I saw you... you were..."

"Oh, this is not my original bodyshell, Master Socket. I have been uploaded to a new one."

The body didn't survive, but Spindle did. "It's not the body that makes the man..."

"But the heart," he finished.

Even though Spindle was a database, technically he didn't *exist,* I still hated it when he broke a body, especially when I did it to him. But he could cheat death by downloading into another body.

"What happened?" I asked.

"I cannot discuss the exercise. The analysis, however, is complete. Pon will discuss the results upon your return."

Bright colors rippled on the surface of his faceplate.

"It's good to see you," I said.

"Thank you for inviting me."

"Inviting you?"

"You invited me to come home," he said. "Do you not remember?"

"Spindle has come along for observation," Mother said. "He wants to experience a public event."

The world was different than it was a year ago. Ever since the Paladins became known, their technology was finding its way into the public like never before. In hindsight, Paladins were behind every major discovery for the last decade. Most people thought Steve Jobs and Bill Gates were Paladins. (They're not.) These days, humanoid mechs, like Spindle, weren't impossible to see in public, it just meant you were sloppy rich. But even the wealthy didn't have humanoid mechs of Spindle's caliber. Spindle could pass for a man. If he had a face.

"Where are you going?" I asked.

"To the tagghet game with you." His eyelight focused on my mother; darker colors stormed his faceplate. "Have you not told him?"

"I wanted it to be a surprise," she said, on her way to the bedroom.

"Are you disappointed, Master Socket?"

"Am I... no! No, I'd love for you to come. I just... uh..."

"What is it?"

"I just was wondering why you're dressed like a commando."

He pulled the hood over his face. The eyelight dimmed until it was difficult to see the featureless aspect of his faceplate. He showed his hand, front then back. The silver tinge sparkled, then darkened to a healthy tan.

"It will lessen the burden of attention. We can enjoy some privacy in the crowd."

He was wearing pants and a shirt, boots and coat in South Carolina. People would avoid us, all right. The cops, however, might want to ask some questions.

"You look psycho," I said.

"Wonderful! I am so looking forward to experiencing a public school tagghet event in South Carolina. I have heard so much about the fans' fervor, and Master Chute is quite good. Currently, she holds the national record for female taggers in assists and single-game goals."

She does?

"She is currently ranked in South Carolina's top ten taggers. It will be quite a joy to see her play tonight, and I know her!" He tilted his head. "I would expect you to know these details about her. She is your girlfriend, after all."

"You're probably right."

"Will Master Streeter be joining us?"

"Ummm... yeah, maybe."

He pumped his fist. "That is great news, also!"

Any other day, Streeter would love sitting next to a humanoid mech. In fact, he'd pull off Spindle's hood and show him off. Now, I don't think he'd give a rat's ass.

"I can prepare dinner," Spindle said. "You may relax, Master Kay."

Mother grinned. "That's all right, Spindle. I'd enjoy doing it myself. I think Socket would like to spend some time with you."

EVEN THOUGH SPINDLE was anatomically neutral, I still preferred he wear something when we sparred, so he stripped down to his shorts. His new body was quicker and stronger. By the time we were done wrestling, my clothes were soaked with sweat and I was aching. It only took three days to lose my edge.

"I like this new bodyshell." Spindle admired his hands. "It seems more capable."

He started doing tai chi in the center of the lawn, where we wore out the grass. His faceplate was frosty, with subtle hints of green. Perhaps the bodyshell was an upgrade, one that knew tai chi. Could I best him in the desert exercise with this one? Would he be crushed against a boulder this time?

"I had a dream after the pre-Trial exercise," I said.

"Oh, really?" he said, striking a pose. "What was it?"

"You had me pinned against the rock, pushing your hand through my shield. You were about to best me."

"That was not a dream."

"Yeah, well, then I saw something else. I saw this kid with his dad. I'd seen them a few days earlier when I went home to see Chute; they were at the tagghet game. But then I dreamed they were there, in the pre-Trial, standing right behind you. He kept asking if I was thirsty."

Spindle turned slowly. "That is very interesting."

"And then the kid's dad turned into my dad."

"Why do you think that is?"

"I don't know. I mean, I only saw the kid for like a second outside the tagghet game. You know what was even crazier? *I was thirsty.* The more I thought about it, the more I wanted a drink."

"And then you saw your father." Spindle stopped the meditative dance. "Perhaps you should investigate how you feel about this dream."

"I would, if I knew what really happened. You were about to beat me, the next thing I saw you smashed against a boulder." I pulled my shirt off and wiped my face. Spindle stood very still. "Maybe you can fill in the blanks."

"I cannot discuss this, Master Socket. Trainer Pon will address the occurrence when you return."

"Occurrence? So something happened."

He tipped his head. He'd already said too much. "I believe it is time to eat."

Spindle was through the door, helping Mom set the table.

Conversation over.

15

BACK IN THE **Game**

I HADN'T SEEN the high school since it was destroyed by the dupli-cates' last stand a year ago. Some of the old live oaks had burned and the reconstruction was expansive. The building was wide, not tall, with green and tan colors that matched the countryside. The walls were made of triple-paned insulated fiberglass that could change colors and opacity, letting in more or less sunlight depending on the season and time of day. The Paladins paid for it all.

I parked far up the road and avoided the traffic. The last thing I needed was the Garrison getting a traffic summons. Besides, Spindle would annoy me all night if I parked illegally. I wanted him to enjoy the game. *I* wanted to enjoy the game.

All Spindle needed was a death sickle to complete the whole grim reaper look, but no one seemed to notice. There were already enough high school freaks to make him look normal. He couldn't get enough of them. *So much culture!*

"This is where you went to school?" Spindle asked.

"That's the place," I said. "I like to think of it as my *prison years.*"

"You were incarcerated?"

"No, it's just what it felt like."

Spotlights beamed up ahead into the low-lying cloud cover, bright enough to illuminate the dusky sky. I avoided walking through the parking lot, where we were sure to find problems. Rednecks, burners, and every other sort of troublemaker would be there. Lookits constantly cruised over the area and reported fights or any other suspicious activity, bringing security as needed, which was at every game. Years ago, it was a prime spot to score weed, speed or meth, but those were the drug days. Now specialized gear could induce a similar high, and no one would know the difference.

The school stadium was on par with Blackbaud. While the color scheme matched the school, it was two stories tall. The outside walls were open scaffolding, and spiraling ramps circled up each corner where people walked to the top.

The crowd funneled toward the main entrance. An arch curved over the gate, swirling with greens and tans and an animated fox mascot clenching his fists at the crowd. A bunch of guys ran past us, bumping into Spindle.

"My apologies," Spindle called.

A couple of them turned around, then turned again. They grabbed their buddies. Thankfully, the rest were too distracted by the girls ahead of them.

"Come on," I said. "We should get inside."

In front of the gates was a low, concrete pond with fountains, where little kids threw coins. A concrete pillar rose from the center of the water with the inscription, *In Memory*. The inscription left out what it was remembering, but everyone knew, they didn't need the words to know all this new stuff was in memory of *those lost in the attack,* when the duplicates launched their first and only public attack.

The fox mascot high-fived the fans. Teachers handed out programs and directed traffic. I didn't bother saying hi. None of the teachers remembered me. As we got closer to the gates, the crowd got tighter. *Look at that* and *it's a humanoid* murmured from those around us, but the line kept moving. We got to the gate without incident, but then a girl tugged on Spindle's hood.

"Hello." His eyelight spun around. "How are you?"

"What are you?"

"I am a—"

I grabbed his sleeve and yanked him onto the pedestrian ramp. "We're going to draw a crowd."

"I just want to be polite."

The girls followed. "Is he yours? What's his name? Hey! Don't be a jag, we just want to see him."

We got up the ramp before they slowed us down. I just wanted to be invisible, which usually wasn't a problem. I should've known this was going to happen.

"He's a prototype," I said. "No big deal."

"Who are you?" the girl said.

"Nobody."

"You don't go to school here, I can tell you that," she said, looking at my white hair.

"You're right."

"I like your coat." One of the girls had a hold of Spindle's sleeve.

"Do you really?" Spindle said. "It came recommended from a website on popular culture…"

"Spindle!" I stood on my toes and tried to whisper. "What're you doing?"

"Your name is Spindle?"

The girls were waving more people over. This needed to be addressed. I flooded their collective awareness with thoughts of boys and cars and food and homework. Their expressions emptied into the storm of pressing thoughts and the emotions that followed. Two seconds later, they were fixated on some boys and forgot they ever saw a one-eyed humanoid.

"From now on," I said, "let's be a little less polite and more invisible."

"I do not want to be rude."

"Just because you don't say hi, that doesn't mean you're rude."

We walked to the top of the ramp and through a short corridor. The stadium seats surrounded the entire field and enclosed skyboxes with black windows looking down from the top. The bleacher seats were steep and filling quickly.

A lookit floated down. *"Do not block corridor."*

I pulled Spindle along like a six-foot kid with attention deficit disorder. The crowd was less rowdy in the seats at the ends of the field, where green scoring cubes hovered off the ground inside bluish domes. We found seats near the top with people that looked like grandparents. Old people couldn't care less about humanoid mechs, and even less about freakishly dressed students. *Perfect.*

I nestled into the soft, moldable seat—no expense spared—and placed a program on the seat next to me, just in case Streeter showed up. A couple had their interactive program open in front of me, watching imbedded vid of their grandson scoring a cube from last season. Spindle's eyelight was bright again, scanning the crowd.

"Explain to me," he said, having to lean his head against mine to be heard over the crowd, "the various subcultures."

I described high school students and how like-minded personalities were attracted to each other and formed group mentalities. There were the gearheads, the bombers, crossers, and brainers, to name a few. I avoided explaining the burners and droppers since they were in the parking lot because then he'd want to know why they weren't supporting the team. I pointed to people I remembered, told him who used to hook up with who and who was popular and who wasn't. And why.

"What about those kids?" Spindle stood and pointed at the band of misfits walking down the aisle, all dressed in black. I yanked him down before they came over and made a scene.

"Those are bleeders," I said.

"They appear to have neck wounds." His eyelight brightened. "If they are not treated, they could become infected."

"Those aren't wounds, just fake tattoos on their necks to look like puncture wounds. It's a whole vampire thing."

"Vampires do not exist."

"Yeah, well, tell them." I stopped him before he did.

"I do not understand. If, in fact, vampires did exist, why would those boys and girls want to walk the earth as the undead?"

"Beats the hell out of me." I smacked his leg. "Kids these days, huh?"

"Which group did you belong to?" he asked.

"None of the above."

"You know what group I believe is right for you?" Spindle crossed his arms, surveying me with his red eyelight. "The potters."

"The what?"

"The potters." His eyelight dimmed, as if squinting. "Surely, there must be a gang of kids that follow the story of Harry Potter, the famous wizard of Hogwarts. It was a worldwide phenomenon."

"And you think I'd be in that group?"

"Why not, Master Socket? I can see it now, you and your friends dressed in your long, flowing robes and knobby wands at your sides, practicing spells between classes..."

"You lost your mind."

I looked over the edge of the stadium while Spindle continued on with his favorite Harry Potter book. I recalled the day when the duplicates attacked the world. I was wearing a dark hoodie, watching Chute in her very first tagghet game.

"You see that over there?" I interrupted Spindle's analysis of Professor Snape. "That's where the truck erupted."

His faceplate sparkled, recalling the incident from his database. He probably had a fully detailed account of the incident from lookit vids that captured the entire ordeal, but he listened to my firsthand account. How the eighteen-wheeled truck caught on fire. How the explosion destroyed the old bleachers and killed people. How the crawlers spewed from the flames like a volcano of freakish spiders, tossing parked vehicles to get to the school's portal underground to let the duplicates have access to virtualmode before they died.

Now, instead of the domed roof, there was a tower encircled with dark windows, like the school was looking in all directions. It was the

Paladins' clever design to remind the public we kept them safe. That we were always watching.

THE CROWD STOOD AND CHEERED. The Hilton Head Hightide rode onto the field on hovering jetter discs, swinging sticks curved at the end over their heads. The self-balancing jetters whizzed at dangerous speeds and the team circled the entire field before huddling at the opposite end.

"*Socket!*" Chute's voice rang in my head. "*Where are you?*"

"On the home team end, behind the goal at the top."

Whatever she said next was blotted out by the roar of the crowd. The Charleston Rapid Foxes blazed onto the field, sticks in the air. Their heads were projected as a hovering three-dimensional image as they hit the field. The players pumped their fists. They were twice as nimble as the last time I'd seen them.

Chute was the last one out and the crowd announced her arrival with an explosion of cheers and the signature *shhhhooooooooot*. Her projected head looked in our direction with a bright smile. I stood on the seat and pulled Spindle up. *Wave, wave*, I told him, and Spindle raised his arms, bright colors dancing inside the hood. She saw us and pointed, but her teammates pulled her into the huddle. I was still standing when the crowd sat. And Spindle was still waving. I pulled his arms down.

They started pregame, doing a double figure-eight and passing three tags. They formed a large line at center pitch and, one at a time, flew toward the goal. Each person cut back and forth with their own display of evasion skills, taking a pass from the sideline and throwing it at the green cube inside the electromagnetized dome. The tag went through the dome and stuck in the cube. Some rode to the top of the dome and fired the tag through it.

Chute worked the jetter like it was an extension of her feet, cutting turns sharply, quickly and precisely. She executed a double-spin move, took the pass blindly with her stick behind her and bounced a shot off the ground that stuck in the center of the cube. *Sweet.*

The crowd was on its feet again.

"Should I wave?" Spindle asked.

"No!" I stood on the seat. "Just shout!"

Fans cupped their hands around their mouths. Spindle put his hands inside the hood and let out a baritone roar that shook the seats, sounding like a goddamn cargo ship. The entire section looked at us.

The energy was exhilarating. I called Streeter and got his voicemail, again.

"Locate." My nojakk reported he was there, at the school, *at the game!* "Where are you?" I said on his voicemail. "Spindle and I are sitting behind the home goal at the top! Get here before the tag drops!"

But as announcements were called and the teams took the field, Streeter's seat was still empty. The announcer's voice was barely audible over the crowd. A lookit hovered over the center pitch with the tag. A player from each team squared off underneath. Holographic numbers counted down over them. On zero, the tag dropped. The stadium shook. Another tagghet season was underway.

I called Streeter again without luck. I wasn't going to leave another message. There was little chance he'd find us in the madness. I called to locate him and get a closer look on his location. I could go get him while Spindle held the seats. He was so fixated on the game, he might not even notice I was gone.

"Locate Streeter." The noise was drowning out the volume in my head. I sat down and covered my ears, calling the command again.

"The recipient's GPS is blocked," it replied.

Streeter shut off his GPS since I left a message. He didn't want me to know where he was.

My neck was beginning to chill.

16

———

Void

Streeter was definitely losing his mind if he thought he could hide from me. Did he forget what Paladins can do?

I activated the imbed and felt it connect with my eyes. I was encouraged not to use it in public because my eyes would be brighter than normal, sometimes even sparkle if it was dark enough.

[Locate Streeter,] I thought.

A virtualmap platform of gridlines stacked in the air, then curved and formed a sphere. Blue oceans and terra firma developed and planet Earth was now rotating in front of me. The Paladin's version of Google Earth was finely detailed, but unlike Google, it was a live feed. The view zoomed into the United States, South Carolina, Charleston, and finally the stadium. A tiny figure was highlighted on the far end of the parking lot.

"Come on."

I pulled Spindle out of his seat and we pushed through the crowd. The imbed locked onto people as we passed and automatically downloaded their history, identifying objects with glowing outlines. Spindle didn't ask questions. He sensed the urgency in my step.

———

WHEN WE ENTERED the parking lot, the burners stared at us; their hair was no longer than mine, but it was knotty, unwashed and hanging in their eyes. One of them blew a long cloud of smoke at us. The distinctive smell of burning skin lingered in the smell of cigarettes, the sort of smell that would emanate from slow-roasting meat. That was the gear cooking their brains, ever so slowly. Most people wouldn't smell that, but most people didn't see what I could see. Or smell.

I didn't recognize any of these people from school, but the imbed immediately downloaded their histories along with names, whereabouts and criminal records. They were mostly small-time punks with dim futures, although some of them were good kids hanging around bad people. Small discs were tucked behind their ears that emitted a low drone and convinced their brains they were happy and good. They were burning on mood gear, cooking their brains like a meth lab.

We were heading for the low-riding black pickup truck parked in the grass with the tailgate down. Streeter had his back to us, talking to a guy with artificially tanned skin. His face was sort of shrink-wrapped over his cheekbones like he'd sucked on the end of a vacuum cleaner.

"This won't take long," I told Spindle.

He slowed his pace and let me approach the truck that reeked of cologne. I reached for Streeter as he put something in the tanned guy's hand.

"What're you doing over here?" I asked.

Streeter jumped back when I touched him and yanked his arm away, breathing heavily. There was another guy sitting on the tailgate that looked lean and dangerous with veins bulging down his forearms. He closed in on me, his muscles tensing. The imbed reported he was a mixed martial artist and a registered bodyguard.

"It's all right, Edward." Vacuumface put his hand up and karateman stopped; then he stared at me for several long seconds, keeping his hand up like he was holding back an attack dog but might change his mind. My reflection looked back from the black sunglasses. Most people wouldn't be able to see with lenses that dark, but he wore them to protect his eyes from light, not to look cool. Even moonlight was too bright for him.

His birth name was Patrick Black and he was a virtualmode dealer, a guy that pushed mood gear to the loitering burners. He was also called a void merchant because he helped people avoid their lives, to get rid of pain and seek pleasure. In reality, he helped them empty their lives until they were void of realness, but his victims wouldn't know what hit them. By the time they were strung out, they wouldn't know the difference between dream and reality. And Streeter was making a deal with him.

Vampires do exist, Spindle.

"My friend," Patrick said, flashing a pearly-white smile, "I'm afraid I only work by appointment. My assistant gets a little nervous when people barge in, you see. You'll have to wait your turn."

"I'm not here to see you. I only need a word with my friend."

"Well, then you and I are mutual friends. Mr. Street and I have spent a lot of time together as of late."

Streeter sort of cringed and turned away.

"My name is Mr. Black." Patrick extended his hand. I didn't shake it. Edward the watchdog twitched. Patrick only smiled.

"No offense, Mr. Black, but I only need a second and I'll be out of your way soon enough."

"No problem. I see you have urgent business and I wouldn't want to be a burden, but you see we're in the middle of an exchange." He held up the item that Streeter had placed in his hand. "Mr. Street has given me something that I desire and I wish to reimburse him for it."

My imbed deciphered the marble as he rolled it up and down his fingers like a magician. What looked like a child's plaything was actually a complex piece of gear that would allow someone to codebreak encryptions. Mr. Black was not likely to use such a device for the betterment of mankind. And Streeter would know that. *Why would he do that?*

"If you'll allow me just a moment to verify the contents," Mr. Black said, "I'll be done before you can lick your lips."

He stared a moment longer. I had the feeling he was staring at my eyes and I was suddenly aware of my imbed's effect on them. Patrick held the marble out to Edward without looking away. Edward took it around to the cab of the truck.

Patrick's cologne stung my nostrils, but it still wasn't strong enough to mask the smell of his burning skin that emanated from tiny discs buzzing behind his ears. His stink was worse than any of the other burners because he'd been doing it for so long. A real veteran of gear addiction, he smelled like summer roadkill.

I turned to Streeter. "You all right?"

He wouldn't look directly at me, but I could see his enlarged pupils and the inflamed ring around his irises. He wasn't in Charleston the other day seeking help. He was with Patrick, but for what? Streeter had everything he needed at home, why would he go to a void merchant? He knew this guy was a new-age heroin dealer, giving his clients free mood discs until they were hooked. Maybe this was more about addiction than his dead parents.

"Mr. Street is quite a talented codebreaker, wouldn't you agree?" Patrick said.

"What're you doing here?"

I didn't mean here in the parking lot or dealing gear. I wanted to know why he bothered leaving virtualmode to come back to his rotting skin. He knew exactly what I meant, but it didn't faze his fake smile. Only made it grow.

"I like to get back to the skin every once in a while," he said. "Mix it up a bit."

More burners were near us, most of them staring at Spindle. They were all teenagers.

"Why don't you go somewhere else, recruit your own kind, not these people," I said. "They're just kids."

"My friend, I don't need to recruit; they line up for my services. Like children at an ice-cream truck. They need what I have."

"You're making them that way."

He frowned. "I haven't done anything. I've only extended my hand; they simply take what's in it."

"You know exactly what you're doing."

"Yes, I do. I'm giving them what they want. Tell me, where is the crime in that? How am I responsible?"

"They don't know what they want."

He gestured to the crowd that seemed to be waiting for us to be done, to have their turn. The smell of smoldering flesh grew stronger.

"Clearly, they do," Patrick said.

Edward came back around and nodded, then fixed his stare on me. Patrick took a red disc from his pocket and held it between his finger and thumb. Streeter reached for it, but Patrick snatched it back.

"We had a deal," Streeter muttered through thin lips.

"I'm curious." He gestured to Spindle. "Tell me about the mech, first."

"He's not for sale," I said.

"I see." He nodded for a while, studying Spindle while he rolled the disc in his fingers, purposely tempting Streeter until he started to fidget. Patrick pushed off the tailgate and circled around Spindle, tugging at the ridiculous overcoat.

I scanned the security lookits through my imbed. Normally, they would've made a few passes through this area by now, but I hadn't seen one since leaving the stadium. It appeared they had been reprogrammed to avoid Patrick while he did business. No doubt, he had the gear to do that sort of thing, so I reset the security paths. One would be around within minutes.

"Very impressive." Patrick peeked into Spindle's hood. "Where do you get one like this?"

"My parents are rich."

"Oh, I've got money, my friend. Surely, you have a price. Everyone has a price."

"I've got everything I need."

"Perhaps your friend has a price?" He went to Streeter and looked down on him. "Mr. Street seems to need something?"

"Listen, there's a lookit coming this way in another minute," I said. "We're done here."

Streeter wasn't about to leave until he got what he came for. And Patrick didn't seem concerned about the incoming lookit, and even less concerned how I knew it was coming.

"You promised," Streeter growled. "I did what you asked, now give it to me."

"Of course, my friend, I will give you what you want. First, I need you to give me what I want."

"I did."

He put his arm around Streeter and stroked his cheek, whispering, "My wants have changed."

I closed in on Patrick. Edward met me there and the four of us stood uncomfortably close like we were about to dance. I pulled Streeter to the side. "We're finished, Mr. Black."

Patrick held up the glittering red disc like a valuable jewel. Streeter was visibly shaking.

"I offer access to dreams," Patrick said.

"Not interested," I said.

"Mr. Street is terribly interested, I'm afraid to say. You see, he wants what I have, what everyone wants." He took Streeter's hand and placed the item in his palm, gently closing his fingers around it. "He wants his heart's desire."

The lookit arrived and did a slow loop overhead, its eyelight pointed at us. Patrick watched it but spoke to me. "You see, I'm doing nothing illegal, my friend. I'm giving people their dreams. Can you do that? Can you make their dreams come true?"

Streeter pushed through the crowd and ran through the parking lot. Patrick pulled his glasses down his nose. His enlarged pupils had nearly swallowed the whites of his eyes, reflecting the headlights behind me. If I could take this guy out, there would just be another one to take his place. How could I argue with him? What people wanted was to fulfill their emotional and physical desires, to get happy and get rid of weakness. To not be afraid. There would always be someone like him to sell that to them, even if the price was steeper than they could ever imagine.

"Maybe we'll meet again, my friend." He flicked his hand at me, as if he'd given me permission to leave.

Spindle and I left the crowd without incident. The scent of charred skin faded behind us. The only way I'd see that cockroach again was if Streeter came back. And I intended to put a stop to that.

17

———————

THE KEY

HOLOGRAPHIC FIREWORKS EXPLODED above the stadium, followed by the announcer shouting above the roar of the crowd.

CHHHUUUUUUUUTTE!

"Wait, Streeter." I caught up to him just as he was leaving the parking lot.

"Go away."

"What're you doing? This isn't like you." I stepped in front of him, but he cut around. "Where are you going?"

"Home."

His lips were tight, and there were too many lines around his eyes. He was lying.

I caught up again. Spindle was trailing behind. "I want to know where you think you're going."

"You deaf? I'm going home."

"No bullshit, Streeter," I said flatly. "Where you going?"

He shut down, marching toward the front of the school with a distant stare.

"What'd Mr. Black give you?"

"Candy. Chocolate-covered candy. Now, can I go home and eat it, or do you want me to share?"

He was squeezing the object in his hand like he was hanging on for his life. I chopped his hand as his arm swung back and the disc dropped in the grass. I picked it up. The center was ruby red, glittering with depth. My imbed read the contents, drawing its data inside and deciphering the code. It was an access key to a moody den in downtown Charleston.

"Give it back."

"Just tell me what's going on." I tossed it back. "I want to help."

"You want to help? Then get out of my way."

"Seriously, just tell me why you're going there." I put my hand on his chest and he finally stopped. "That's all I want to know."

He rubbed the ruby center with his thumb and sighed, looking off in the distance. Maybe it was my touch, or just someone finally caring about where he was at and what he was going through.

"It's just a gear booster, that's all," he said. *Lie.* "My home gear is junking, I need more dataflow to, you know, go to that one... place."

"Back to the gates?"

He nodded.

"I thought you were going to get help?"

"I will," he said. "After."

"I don't think you should go."

"Yeah, well, it's my life."

"That's a key, Streeter. It's not a gear booster."

"Then why'd you ask? Look, if you want to stop me, fine; go ahead and stop me. I don't give a fuck because in another week you'll be gone and I'll go get another one." He threw the thing at me. "Keep that for a souvenir."

"How can you do this? That guy's a void merchant. You'll be hooked."

"I'll take the chance."

"You want to be one of them?"

He rubbed his eyes with the heel of his hand. "I got to do what I got to do."

I dropped my hand and he didn't run. He just stared down.

"You don't know what that's like," he said. "I got to see my parents and I'll do whatever I got to do."

The key twinkled, like it agreed.

"Your parents are gone, Streeter. You're still alive; don't do this to yourself. You got to let it go."

He looked off to the side and sort of laughed. "Man, I at least thought *you'd* understand."

"My old man is gone, Streeter. I know that. I don't need to spend time on a memory. You got to face the facts, you're addicted to gear. Don't let a memory ruin your life."

He was nodding and, for a moment, looked like he was considering what I said. He was trying to go somewhere that didn't exist anymore. He was trying to go back home, back to a time when he was a little boy and his mom and dad were still around. But that was a memory and he was here and now. He couldn't throw his life away for something that didn't exist.

"Give me the key, I'll use it now or I'll get one for later. Either way, I'm going and you can't stop me. It's my life. Go live your own."

"Forget it." I clenched my fist. "I'll assign a Paladin sentry wherever that key leads. I'll send doctors to your house, if that's what it takes. I'm not letting you do it."

I couldn't do any of those things. He knew it.

His energy swirled darkly around him with waves of blue and violet, saturated with grief. His chest heaved.

"I don't have anyone," he whispered. "You know that? I'm all alone. I just got some things to say to my folks, that's all. I know that doesn't make sense to you, you don't have to feel, but I… I do. I just think, maybe, things will be easier if I see them one last time. That's all I'm asking."

"This is wrong; you need help. I know it stinks, but sometimes the right thing smells like shit."

"If it smells like shit," he said, "it's shit, Socket."

Halftime had arrived and it seemed like half the crowd was walking past us, laughing and having a good time, but whispering after they passed. They recognized Streeter, the school's virtualmode king, the number one codebreaker, slumped over on the front steps with some white-haired stranger and a goofy trench-coat man. *Stranger.* Is that what I'd become? A cold-blooded asshole?

He wiped his nose and eyes.

The facts were this: He was going. Now or later. I'd rather be with him if he was going to do this. I could protect him if I was there, but if he went alone, there was no telling what would happen.

"Promise you'll get help after this?" I held up the key.

He nodded.

"I mean real help. Like a family counselor and gear-addiction therapy. I mean it, I'll tell my mother to send the best doctors."

"Yeah," he said, nodding, looking up. "Yeah, I'll do it."

I sent Spindle to fetch the car.

Streeter sat on the step, deflating with relief. I stood in front of him, warding off stares of curiosity, until the black sedan pulled up.

18

———

Judgment Day

There wasn't a lot of talking.

Streeter sat in the passenger seat. His fingers twittered on his leg like his hand was trying to run away. In the window's reflection, his eyes didn't look at anything in particular.

It was stop-and-go traffic until we reached downtown's historic marketplace, a long narrow building that extended for blocks, where vendors peddled T-shirts, fragrance and sweetgrass baskets to cash-heavy tourists. I found parking halfway down the market in front of an outdoor café, the exact one Chute and I were destined for a week earlier. Streeter sat quietly. Fingers running.

"You sure you want to do this?" I asked.

He nodded and got out.

"Stay here." I turned to Spindle in the backseat. "Pull the hood tight and don't move. Stay vigilant. I'll be back as soon as possible."

"Yes, Master Socket."

I locked the car. Streeter was fidgeting on the curb. "You know where we're going?"

"There's a moody club around the corner. The virtualmode den is in the back."

"We're not old enough."

He held the disc between his fingers. "We are now."

Streeter led the way. We worked our way around tourists gawking through windows and licking gigantic ice cream cones. We got to the end of the market and turned the corner, where bars and restaurants lined the street, the doors open to the sidewalk.

A five-star hotel was on the corner. Nothing but suits and dresses sat in the first-floor restaurant with padded menus that didn't have prices. Next door, techno music thumped where singles got their freak on. Sandwiched in-between the five-star restaurant and techno bar was a door with peeling red paint. A barrel-shaped man sat on a stool in front of this door.

Streeter held out the disc. It took the man a moment to even see him. He scrunched his face like he was about to tell him to beat it until he saw the disc. He looked twice, thought about smacking Streeter for the hell of it, then pressed the disc into the palm of his glove. He handed it back and simply nodded.

Above the red door, in small, old-school neon lights, was a sign. *Judgment Day.* Behind the door was a flight of stairs. Streeter took a hesitant step inside and I followed. The door slammed behind us, sealing out the traffic and music like a tomb. The stairwell smelled like five hundred years of mold and made my head light as if memories of the building tried to get inside me. A single light bulb hung at the top of the steps. Someone had gouged *Stairway to Heaven* into the first step.

The walls were smeared with graffiti. Most were names immortalized with the tip of a knife or a Sharpie, or just statements of who loved who forever and ever. Then there was one that hit me. *Paladins Feed on the World.* And if that wasn't clear enough, *Paladins Suck Ass.*

I wanted to put my fist through the wall. Without the Paladin Nation, the world would be dead. And they embraced the enemy? Pon's voice echoed from somewhere deep in my brain.

We don't ask for permission to serve.

At the top of the steps, another man on another stool. Not as round, but just as big. He stared at us all the way to the top. Streeter held out the disc. He pressed it to his glove without taking his eyes off Streeter.

He nodded, then held the disc up like a communion wafer. Streeter, unsure, plucked it from his fingers. The guy didn't move. The door behind him was old and peeling, too, but this one had a crystal doorknob. Streeter put his hand on it, turning it slowly. *Heaven's inside.*

The room inside was reddish, long and narrow. A bar was along the left wall. A bartender leaned on the polished surface; another guy was on a barstool. His tie was loose. He had no drink.

Booths were along the right, filled with people. Most were young, some were locals. They had their fingers dipped in a black saucer in the center of each table. Some had their heads back, some slumped over, their eyes glassy and aimless. *Moody bowls.* Unlike the moody discs Patrick was dealing, moody bowls were legal mood enhancers. *The body's natural opiate. Make life feel better, dip into a moody bowl today.*

The government ruled years ago that moodies were no more dangerous or addictive than a cup of coffee. "It's just a little escape," the woman in the commercial used to say, with her frizzy hair and crying baby. "Who doesn't need a vacation now and then?" She looked back at the baby, then put her thumb in a small moody bowl. Her eyes closed. "I know I do."

The booths had teenagers and adults, some with clothes that needed washing, and others looked like lawyers or doctors. They could've been my next-door neighbors. Escape had them mesmerized, escaping whatever they were running from. They tricked the brain to boot out good feelings, that the world was all right, just like it was when they were kids watching their favorite show. *I love you, you love me...*

The crowd in the middle of the room was more sophisticated. They belonged in a five-star restaurant instead of the moody den. They sat at elevated tables or stood in groups, swaying to the soft notes of a piano playing somewhere in the back. They smiled and laughed, speaking in hushed tones. They all looked around every few seconds, like they were waiting for something.

We politely worked our way around the tables and between the well-to-do people that ignored us like kitchen help. One lady grabbed my hair and let it fall between her fingers. "Nice hair," she said. Her pupils were enlarged, but she still had irises. Not yet a void, but on her way.

There was a doorway on the back wall and a silver podium facing it. A woman walked out of the doorway as if the archway was a solid outline on the wall. *Like Garrison technology.* A gentleman and his date shoved past us without an apology. He placed a disc similar to Streeter's on the podium. The silver surface absorbed it and the doorway started glowing. The couple rushed through it.

Streeter approached the podium next. There was no one stopping him. He did like the guy before him and the doorway responded. He took a deep breath and looked back, then walked through it like a curtain of water. Gone.

I went through the cold archway and stepped next to Streeter into a tiny elevator room. There was slight nausea in my belly and the atmosphere became slightly more humid and cooler. The wall lit again.

This is a leaper! They have access to Paladin technology!

Streeter took another long breath, but I stepped through the lit wall first.

THIS ROOM WAS gray and damp, mold in the corners, big enough for a bunk bed and two chairs. The stench shot up my nose, like something rotten hovered just below a heavy dose of sterilizing solution. The mattresses were bare with large yellowish stains. Stains layered upon stains. Empty life-support jacks on the wall were options for long-term virtualmode living, lines that would pump nutrition into veins for weeks, months or however long a client's bank account held up.

Putrid memories haunted the room. No joy ever remained, yet the promise of such was always present.

"I know what you're thinking," Streeter said, his voice wavering. "But I'm not here for a long trip." He sat in a chair, sinking in as the ultra-molding pads reformed to his body.

"You're not using their transporters, are you?"

"I have to." He took two discs off the table between the chairs and slid a transparent film over them. "But this will sterilize them."

He was lucid enough, not too desperate, to realize that transporters in a void-ridden place like this would have leacher technology that gave the user a *taste* of that connection and left him wanting more. People thought heroin was addictive? Try leacher gear that left an imprint on your brain, like a permanent brand with instructions to come back for more. No cure for that and guaranteed repeat customers. Ask those that pissed on the mattresses.

"I've got extra sterilizers for you," he said.

"No, thanks." I tapped the back of my neck. "I've got an imbed."

Under normal circumstances, he'd want to know everything about imbed technology. He'd heard of it, so what was it like? When could he get it? But he didn't flinch. He pressed the transporters behind his ears and lay back. Unlike the moody discs that the burners placed behind their ears, the transporter discs pulled Streeter's awareness from his skin into virtualmode. I sat in the chair —the remnant energy of all the addicts that sat in it before me crawled over my skin like ants—and activated my imbedded portal.

I LEFT my skin and arrived at the Gates of the Dead. Streeter was already there. For the first time ever, he was in a sim that looked like his actual skin body, back when it was plump and healthy. I felt hopeful.

Leaves crunched under my feet. I stepped next to him, looking into the black depths between the bars.

"I didn't plan on this happening." His gaze was blank. "But when I saw them..." He swallowed.

"I understand." I didn't understand, but he needed to hear that.

"When I saw them, something snapped inside me." Focus returned to his eyes. "You ever seen your dad?"

I shook my head.

"You should try it," he said. "It'll fuck you up, bro."

The gates opened. The blackness behind them swirled and details took shape. Streeter took one deep breath and marched through them. Grass sprouted under our feet. Live oaks from before the time of the Civil War lined the large expanse of turf. Traffic cruised outside of that. Tourists were looking over the wall at crashing waves, and a barge loaded with containers slowly cruised into the harbor. We were standing at Battery Park, right downtown, where tourists could see Fort Sumter across the harbor.

Streeter was stoic, eyes fixed straight ahead. The park was filled with the usual crowd. A couple college guys were tossing a Frisbee and some kids were throwing food to the seagulls. Streeter watched it like a movie.

"This world is addictive." He held out his hands, turning them over. "The details are better than anything I've ever seen. I can smell the ocean and feel the breeze, like I'm really here. You start to forget what's real."

"The Battery is just three blocks away in the skin. Let's get out of here and go."

He pointed. "They won't be there."

On the far side of the park, a couple was holding hands. They walked at a leisurely pace. I recognized them from a picture in Streeter's house; it sat on a shelf in the den, right above his grandfather's desk. Streeter was two years old, sitting on the beach with the tide rushing in. His dad had curly hair and a big round face, what his grandfather called swarthy. His mother had blond hair and her lips were red; she smiled big and there was lipstick smudged on her teeth.

Streeter always said that was his favorite picture. I never knew why, it wasn't all that flattering, but then after a while I got it: It was real. Nothing pretend about it; those were real people with their son at the beach. The same two people walking across the park.

"You see, this is where the trip always ends," Streeter said. "I see them across the park." His father, still a hundred yards out, waved at us. "They wave. Then it ends, the world goes black and I end up back at the gates, starting all over. You know what it would cost for me to get closer?"

"By the look of that crowd in the lobby, I'd say half a million."

"Close." His lower lip started to tremble. "The security of this world is tight, I couldn't hack my way past that point without paying, and I ain't got half a mil cooling in my pocket. And once I got a taste, I couldn't stop. I went night after night, trying to codebreak the security, just so I could get a little closer, but I couldn't pull it off. I stripped the safety features off my gear. I know it's dangerous—that I've started gear addiction. I stopped going to school because if Mr. Buxbee saw me, he'd lock me up. I'll go to detox, Socket, I swear I will. But not until after."

They were fifty yards out. His mother waved this time. Streeter made an odd sound, like he got punched in the stomach, started to reach for his face, and seemed unsure about what to do.

"I made a deal with the devil, Socket. I wrote some difficult code to get this key and Mr. Black is going to use it to rob some innocent people with it. But I had to, you understand?" His eyes were wet. "I just had to."

I squeezed his shoulder. *I understand.*

He took a step, slow and frightened that the trip would end. When the ground was still under his feet, he took another. On the third, he was running. His parents put their arms out. Streeter crashed into them. He buried his face between them, his body convulsing. They hugged him tight, held him an arm's distance away like long-lost ones trying to see what their boy had become. Streeter was trying to talk, but just made weird sounds. He was in a full-on meltdown.

I was feeling it, too. I felt guilt mixed with relief. Guilt for not understanding. Relief he found what he needed. Guess there was a lot more buried in him than I thought.

Flicker.

The world crinkled.

I grabbed a bench for support. Streeter was still there. His parents, too. But the traffic was gone, so was the water.

Flick, fiililckkkk.

I lost contact with my sim, floating in the in-between. I pulled my awareness back into my skin and sat up. My nostrils had soured in the room's rancid odor. Streeter was still in virtualmode, tears streaming down his face. The doorway to the leaper was glowing.

"Socket?"

"Chute!" I touched my nojakk cheek.

"Is Streeter all right?"

His lips were moving, tears still flowing. "Yeah," I said. "He's going to be all right."

A cold chill leaked down my neck, voices gurgling. My body was alight with tension, the timeslicing spark dancing in my belly. I shook my head to clear the confusion. I couldn't leave Streeter, but I was pulled in forty directions. I bent over, closed my eyes and held my head together. Chute was saying something.

"...glad Streeter's with you. Where are you?"

I was going to answer. I was thinking of meeting her down at the market, at the outdoor café. Streeter, maybe he would be up for telling her about it. We could reconnect, all three of us.

The chill froze my neck, harder than ever.

The voices.

Heeee's in there is what it said. Or maybe Chute said it.

"What?" I answered.

Chute said something, but I couldn't hear through the voices. I needed to hear what that cold chill was telling me. It was Streeter's voice; was he speaking on the nojakk? No, it was... from somewhere else, some time else...

CRACK-flash.

It was a blunt object. A club.

The back of my head.

I sensed it, at the last second, and tried to slow time. But the world spun.

My face numb.

I had face-planted into the floor. Blood gushed through my lips to the back of my throat. There were people in the room, like a dozen, swimming back and forth. I couldn't count them all. Maybe three. I just couldn't... focus. I flopped over; Streeter was in the chair, oblivious to what was going on. I squeezed time to stop it, but couldn't get a grip. There was little feeling in my body.

A tanned face hovered over me. "Hello, friend," he said, his voice far away. "You didn't think I could smell a fucking Paladin?"

I tried to sit up, but the bottom of a boot knocked me down. The back of my head exploded on the floor.

Time?

There was only a brown face in front of me. No details. No room. Just a smudgy face. Someone spat. Something wet splattered on my cheek. "We don't fear the Paladin Nation."

My lips were too fat, but they tried, quaking and bubbling. Couldn't get them to work. I couldn't utter a single word, couldn't send a single lucid thought to Spindle sitting safely in the car. Couldn't do anything but let the dead silence of my confusion flounder. I managed a sound, but it was nothing.

"Call all you want." The face receded. "We've isolated your communications. No nojakk, no thoughts, no nothing. It's just you, now. Deep underground. You're in our world, friend. And you're not going home. Not tonight."

My lips, fat and bloated, split as I smiled. *They cut my communications.*

Commotion in the room.

My communication is my lifeline. If there's no lifeline...

Something crashed on the wall. A body fell over me.

Screams.

He hears my heartbeat.

Silence.

When he can't hear it...

A silver face hovered over me.

...he comes.

"We are leaving, Master Socket."

19

―――――

Drown

IT WAS like a throbbing metal rod had been rammed up my nose. Pain and pressure rhythmically spread over my face.

The bridge of my nose, broken. My cheek, fractured. They had to secure two of my front teeth and reattach nerves along with bone mending. I was told that was what happened on the first day. I only remembered half of the second. On the third day, I woke to the brutal reality of a broken face.

"You have been denied pain control," they told me. "Orders from Trainer Pon."

Pon still hadn't returned from Pike's relocation, but he was giving orders. There was no explanation with them, but then again there didn't need to be. *Deal with pain.* Oh, and that was what you get for being a fuckup. You get pain. *I told you that you can't go home. Should've listened.*

I SAT up in bed and my sinuses swelled. I paused before my face exploded. Mother could override this order to keep me in pain if she took it high enough, but then what? I had to deal with it on my own, that was what Pon was teaching me. I started to grind my teeth, resisting Pon's apparent wisdom, but this only sent a spike through my brain. I don't know what I hated more: When Pon was right, or when it hurt this much. *Both.*

I took a cup of water from the nightstand without leaning over. I wasn't sure if I had the balance to keep myself upright if my momentum started in any one direction. My throat was parched from breathing through my mouth. I chugged the water in three gulps.

What a joke.

I was nearly destroyed by a goddamn void merchant, a piece of shit that rarely came back to the skin. Face it, if Spindle wasn't there, they never would've found me. And Pon was training me to go into the world to save it? *I can't even save myself.*

No matter how much I wanted to deny it, I was still human. I still had emotions and I was still fucked up. Maybe I was too hard on Streeter. I mean, I got every expert in the world, maybe the universe, to help me deal with daily problems, and look at me: I'm racked up in the infirmary. Streeter was on his own, dealing with emotions that didn't make sense the only way he knew how. And not just Streeter, all those burners in the parking lot and those people dipping into a moody bowl, they just wanted to ease the pain and emptiness of life, that was all. What chance did those people have if I was still an idiot with a more evolved race of humans at my disposal?

Pain is part of life, Pon would say. *There's much to learn from it.*

Once my head found peace with the upright position, I touched my feet on the floor and eased my weight forward. The pulsing pain diminished. It was getting from horizontal to vertical that hurt.

I was in a one-bed infirmary with a single window. The view was projected from the side of the Garrison's sheer-face wall that faced the wormhole that led back to South Carolina. The sun was high and the grass shivered in the breeze. I asked Mother for the view. I needed something that would remind me of the way home because I was pretty sure I'd never see it again.

"The commander is very disappointed," she told me.

She had paced at the foot of my bed. I'd let the commander down. Let the Paladin Nation down. Worst of all, I let her down. She trusted me.

"You went into a known duplicate-sympathizing club *with Streeter!*" she said. "How irresponsible!"

The graffiti. The leaper. And the bouncer at the top of the steps was running an imbedded portal. And Patrick? Those weren't headlights I saw reflecting in his pupil-engorged eyes, that was a sparkling imbed. He knew exactly who I was and where I came from the second I arrived.

I should've aborted the whole thing, but no one was going to understand. Streeter was going in there and I wasn't stopping him. I took a chance and failed. Streeter's life was not worth the life of a Paladin cadet, my superiors might believe. Ordinary people were as common as raindrops. A Paladin was rare. Do the math, Socket. You made the wrong choice.

"Streeter?" I had asked. "He's okay, right?"

Mother had stopped her pacing. "Yes."

"Can I talk to him?"

"You are not allowed communication with Streeter. Or Chute."

The emptiness of her expression spoke volumes. Pon had total control now. She once had the advantage, but that was long gone now. *You're too emotionally involved, Kay. You will be allowed to check on Socket, but Pon now has complete authority to squash him like a mosquito. Sorry about that, but it's his fault.*

Pon's first order: a heaping dose of pain. Let Socket reap the harvest of his mistake and feel each nerve cry. And forget about home. Not even pictures. All he gets is training, starting now. Welcome home to that.

Spindle entered the room. "How are you feeling?"

"Fantastic."

He was back to wearing the purple overcoat swishing around his ankles. He held my face gently with both hands. "Let me take a look," he said.

His eyelight cruised over my face. He touched the back of my head and let his fingertips softly brush over my cheeks. A few colors danced in his faceplate while he evaluated my recovery. I could see my reflection. Purples and blacks darkened my eyes and my nose had doubled in size. I looked like I'd kissed a train.

"Have you heard from Chute and Streeter?" I asked.

"Mmmm." He continued examining. "They have sent messages."

"Will I see them?"

"Pon will not release them."

"What'd they say?"

"Streeter is getting help for his gear addiction. He thanked you a dozen times, Master Socket, and apologized for getting you in trouble another dozen." His eyelight focused on my eyes. "He is truly grateful for your friendship."

Then the facelift was worth it.

"Chute is thankful, as well," he said. "She cannot wait to see you."

Maybe Pon should let her know that'll never happen. I doubt Spindle should've summarized the messages, but maybe Pon wasn't specific about not telling me what the message was.

"She set a state record that night," Spindle said. "She scored a single game high for scores. I believe that should make you proud. She is quite an athlete."

Maybe Pon was right, it was better I didn't hear these things. It hurt worse than my face.

"Well, then." Spindle stepped to the doorway. "Your healing is coming along nicely, although a bit painful, I believe."

"The understatement of the year," I said, trying not to move my lips.

"Trainer Pon would like to see you in the training room."

"Now?"

"Time is scarce. The Realization Trial will not be rescheduled. You have fifteen days."

If it wasn't apparent no one was doing me favors yet, it was now. Train, no matter how swollen your face.

———

I was in the middle of the training room, again, waiting for the teacher to appear. This time with my nerve endings on fire.

It hurt to have my hair pulled back in a ponytail, so I let it hang over my face. Forget awareness and the present moment, I just wanted the pain to go away. Standing at attention was not helping.

Maybe Pon would understand. I was helping someone in need. Okay, so I fucked things up, but I'm still a cadet. We could put the scenario back together; it would give me a chance to analyze it.

I paced around, trying to stay one step ahead of my thoughts, but they trailed behind like cans tied to strings. I focused on breathing, letting the thoughts rise and drift, but there were so many of them. Thoughts about Streeter and Chute, Pon and this godforsaken place. The weight of the mountain felt like it was sitting squarely on my chest. I took a deep breath, but the pressure wouldn't let up.

Pon popped out of the floor and startled me. I went back to the center, where I should've been. I blew at my hair hanging over my eyes.

He was rigid. His hands were not behind his back but crossed over his chest. And his posture was slightly askew, his shoulders thrown back a few degrees. I expected utter disappointment on his face, perhaps disgust. But he was void of any of that. He was expressionless.

He gazed at my midsection. Pon rarely looked anywhere but my eyes. They revealed more than any word or movement. His gaze was unfocused, slightly hazy. Deep in thought.

"When I was twelve," he said, "I watched three boys drown."

What?

He swung his foot to the side, took three paces, turned, and paced back.

"Perhaps they swam too far out into the ocean or a riptide carried them, it did not matter. Their heads were barely above the water and they were waving for help. I imagine they were calling, but I could not hear their voices over the surf. One second I could see them, the next they would disappear behind a wave and then they were back."

He stopped at the end of his pacing and bounced the tips of his splayed fingers in front of his chest.

"I calculated how far out they were, the weight of their bodies and the energy I would need to bring them back. I knew I was not capable of saving them, and had I gone, I would have drowned as well. So I watched them bob in the ocean until they did not reappear."

The pain receded in my focus. Something wasn't right.

"There was quite a commotion after their deaths. The community was saddened and I felt disgusted with my inaction. But as the days passed, I realized guilt was a useless emotion. I could not save those boys. My death would not have justified their deaths anymore than standing there. And how I felt about it, how anyone *felt* about it, was pointless."

"You could've tried."

He stopped mid-stride. "You cannot save everyone, cadet."

"I'm saving the ones that want to be saved."

He nodded, but still looked at the floor. He resumed his one-man parade.

"The Paladin Nation has asked that I terminate your training. Your failure to act responsibly and capably was reprehensible. You are not fit to be a Paladin, regardless of your aptitude."

"Fine."

"You believe it is that simple, mmm? That you can return to your former life? You would prefer that?"

I didn't answer.

The room shifted, forming objects and colors and bodies. A long bar took shape to my left and booths on the right. Men and women emerged at elevated tables around us, all frozen in a lifeless moment.

The Judgment Day club had been resurrected to the very moment I had entered it with Streeter. Pon stood in front of a woman and touched her face. She was the one that touched my hair.

"This woman identified you as a Paladin cadet and confirmed your identity. A year of training and you could not assess this simple action? You cannot perform a simple task on your own?" He brushed the wrinkles from her shoulders carefully. "You will not waste any more of my time."

"Then be done with me."

"Even now, you react. You let your emotions guide you."

"Maybe those kids wouldn't have drowned if you did the same."

"If I did the same, I wouldn't be here today to save you."

"Maybe one of them would."

He looked at me for a second. His eyes were glassy. He looked away, pacing between the still-formed crowds; the reddish light from the bar cast strange color onto his cheeks.

"You cannot act upon what feels good or bad, cadet. Emotions will betray you."

"I should be a calculator, is that it?" I said. "Add up the numbers and see what lives are worth saving and which ones aren't. How much is a Paladin life worth, Pon? Ten ordinary people? Twenty? You need to give me that formula so I'll know when it's worth swimming out."

"There's no formula. As I have trained you for the past year, the present moment contains all existence. Just listen. Learn to listen to the present moment, do not tell it how you feel about it."

I slammed my fist on a round table, spilling a drink. "I DID WHAT THE MOMENT REQUIRED!"

"Your friend is responsible for his own life."

"He needed help."

"You failed," Pon said simply.

"I saved a life, isn't that what we're trained to do?"

He picked up the fallen glass and gently placed it on the table. "Your friends will forget you."

"They won't."

"You will become a ghost in their memories. They will recall a childhood friend, but they will not remember your face. They will not remember the sound of your voice or the touch of your hand."

"She won't forget."

"You are slipping from the memories of all that knew you, shedding your old life, preparing for a new one. Your loved ones will be the last to hold onto that memory, but even they will forget. In the end, you will be alone."

Pressure gripped my chest. I forced myself to breathe.

"You cannot have attachments. Would you have saved your friend if you did not know him?"

No, I wouldn't walk a stranger up to that room. But what if they were all strangers? What if no one remembered me, who did I save then? How did I decide?

The energy in the room shifted. Pon walked past me with his hands at his sides. His gait changed. The steps became shorter, his balance lowered. Tension rippled up his arms, over his shoulders. I brushed the evolvers on my belt, turned my hips toward him and analyzed the room and the contents for position. Pressure clamped my chest; my breath wheezed in my throat. *Is this an exercise?*

"Do you know what it feels like to drown?" Pon paused at the bar. "There is panic, at first, when you realize that death is imminent. Thoughts seize the muscles. You fight to stay above the water until exhaustion sets in. You sink a few times and come up for air, perhaps take in water, until you no longer have the strength to stay above the surface."

He walked along the bar; each step was purposeful, his fingers curved like claws. I turned so he would not see my back.

A man leaped from the booth behind me. I shifted my weight, caught his arm and tossed him across the room.

"You hold your breath, at first, try to make the air in your lungs last, fighting the water that pushes on your lips. But your lungs contract."

The bartender pulled a gun from below. The evolver unfolded around my arm and a burst of blue energy shot from my open hand, melting the barrel and half his arm.

"A fire burns the hungry cells in your lungs."

I kicked the tables away, clearing space. With both evolvers, I crouched in the center of the room.

"Your head swells painfully."

All the glassy-eyed patrons with their fingers stuck in the moody bowls attacked. I cut away their knees with a long stroke of a blue saber. Blood splashed the walls.

"Water, the very substance that gives you life, now takes it."

One man eluded my counterattack and got close enough to bring a glowing dagger down on me. I activated a shield and inserted a knife between his ribs. *Why am I slaughtering these people?*

"The useless air is expelled from your lungs and you choke soundlessly. You thrash helplessly. You sink." Pon walked behind a small group of men in tuxedoes. "Inevitably."

He did not emerge on the other side. Instead, Streeter appeared. His hands were glowing with evolvers. His eyes were dark and angry. Vengeful.

"Save me, Socket," he said.

He took a step, then another, and then leapt, hands above his head, a long spear aimed for my chest. My heart thumped inside, aching to be released from the building pressure. It needed space. It wanted out.

I dodged to the left, using an impact pulse to launch Streeter across the room. His frail body cracked into the wall, falling over the back of a booth at a broken angle.

I couldn't get enough air. My chest squeezed my lungs smaller and tighter. *I'm suffocating.*

"Sometimes you have to let them drown." Pon was behind me.

I spun. He was gone again.

"You have to surrender."

I screamed, shoving tables and bodies away, blasting them against the walls until I was the only thing standing.

Pon's bodiless voice spoke. "You have to *die!*"

I rolled sideways, ignited a shield from my left hand and sprayed bursting projectiles blindly behind me. Pon moved deftly, his motions animal-like, lanky and graceful, blocking my shots and advancing. I jumped onto the booths and swiped at him with a three-headed whip, a sweeping line that he bent his body around. The whips carved through the floorboards.

Our shields clashed and our weapon hands locked together. I had the advantage from above, careful not to overcompensate that he might shift and toss me. He was stuck in the corner. Maybe it was the weight of my chest or the adrenaline or his exhaustion, but I overpowered him. I forced him into a compromised position. His neck was prone.

I would best him.

Spit shot from his lips and he pulled me closer, the tip of my weapon closing in on his neck. He wanted me to win. I smelled his breath and looked into his eyes.

His eyes.

The depth, the steel, was gone. This was not the man that had trained me. There was something else in his eyes, someone familiar. From another time. It was the eyes of another man. An enemy I once knew. That was not Pon inside.

It felt like... *impossible.*

I pressed the tip of my weapon closer, touching the throbbing artery on his neck. His eyes were wide open, as if begging me to look inside.

Pon is the greatest trainer of all time.

He leaned forward, my dagger sizzling on his skin with no regard for life or death. He wanted me to see.

My mentor.

The smell of burnt flesh wafted up. I pulled the dagger back. Leaned closer.

Closer to see.

It wasn't Pon inside. It was a predator. A deceiver. I saw inside... *PIKE.*

Pon is a pawn!

Pon/Pike hooked his leg around mine, twisted his hips and turned me on my back. I was flung hard into the wall.

White light exploded in the back of my already thumping head. I squeezed the shield to full strength with both hands.

Pon's face was inches from mine, but Pike's eyes bore down. The tip of a dagger pushed through my shield and touched my throat. Now it was my jugular throbbing against a deadly edge. His eyes were tunnels that reached deep into a shell of a man that guided me through my training, that had been with me through my development, the man that prodded me to grow, to realize. At the very end was a vengeful puppeteer. A master of psychic manipulation. Pike had defeated Pon. Through him, he would defeat me.

"No." I shifted my weight, squeezed the shield tighter, pushed the dagger back, but he found renewed strength to force the weapon closer to my neck. His lips pulled back over his teeth. I could not stop him.

"NO!" My chest resisted the pressure inside. There was nowhere to go. Nothing I could do to stop him.

"Your father was a pig." His voice was hardly recognizable, beaten and hoarse. "Pigs do not go to battle. Pigs go to slaughter."

I expected the killing blow to be cold and quick like a shank that would slice through my throat. But instead, there was an explosion from deep in my chest. My heart had been set free, destroying the steel cage that imprisoned it. I heard nothing. Saw nothing.

And there was great relief.

Tremendous freedom.

I fell onto the floor, exhausted. Full surrender. Complete liberation.

Everything was broken. Across the room, slumped against the wall, was the body of Pon, buried into a depression like he'd been driven into it. It was limp and lifeless. It didn't match the vision that I had when I was with Com, but the details were irrelevant.

That is not Pon.

Newfound life crackled through me, fueled by bitterness and hatred. I snapped open my hands; blue flames flickered in my palms. I would smite this traitor from the world, take this unholy affliction from the face of the earth. No more people would drown because of him. No more death. *NO MORE!*

I pushed off the wall, soaring across the room. Hands together, above my head. Long, broad swords emerged to impale the heart of evil. Anger shook my body, thirsting for the salty tang of his blood. The death this world deserved.

I was hit with a detainment wire. Another line wrapped around my midsection like a thin snake and another around my arms and legs. I crashed into the manufactured bodies piled against the wall and carelessly cut the lashes from my skin with the evolver, searing deep wounds in my calves and elbows.

"*NO!*" I cried.

My evolvers yelped with power, drawing from the depths of my rage. Fireballs melted the first spidery crawler guard that appeared. I destroyed a second one preparing to fire another detainment line, but more entered the room. I slashed and burned them, but they overwhelmed me with numbers. The cool, silky lines encased me.

"Master Socket." Spindle knelt next to me.

"He's a traitor, Spindle! That's not Pon, that's Pike! Look in his eyes! PIKE IS CONTROLLING HIM! KILL HIM NOW!"

Spindle took my head with both hands, but I thrashed him away. He took my head again and again until the healing vibrations from his palms sank deeply. I strained against the constraints, hissing through my teeth. Several crawlers huddled around.

I let myself fall limp. Breathing came easier. The traitor was only five feet away. I could do nothing. But when I looked between the crawlers' spindly legs, there was only an indention.

Pon's body was missing.

"He's gone," I muttered. "You let him get away."

"Pon has been transported to the infirmary. The impact has caused him great harm."

Impact?

The commander's voice resonated inside the room. Others were with him. Spindle had both hands on my chest, sending healing warmth inside me. My body was so empty and depleted. The colors on his faceplate ran wild. I grabbed his wrist, unable to squeeze, suddenly aware of the complete exhaustion. Barely able to whisper, I asked, "What happened?"

"Master Socket," he said, his eyelight looking at me, "you are telekinetic."

20

THE EDGE

THEY SUBDUED me after the attack. I slept for days. I woke with my legs bandaged where I tried to cut away the crawler guards' detainment lines. When they released me from the infirmary, it wasn't without a fight. I rebelled by trashing the room, demanding to see Pon, or Pike, or whoever the fuck he was. I blamed the meds they gave me for that freak-out, some stuff that was supposed to keep me calm and relaxed and open to understanding. I understood, all right. Understood I wanted to wreck something and everything in that room was the winner.

I didn't see a live person that day, only servys. The next day, I settled down. Minders came in to do some tests, penetrate my mind and body, see how I was holding up. They did their job like usual, with confidence that bordered on arrogance, but they were hiding a quiver of fear. They saw what happened to Pon/Pike. If I could do that to him... so they tread lightly, like a bomb squad.

Spindle was the only one acting normal. He refused to talk about the incident, citing the commander's orders. This went on for days and it only pissed me off. I think I trashed the room again. But then it was clear they were going to keep me until I got a hold of myself. It took some effort and a couple of days of meditation, but I disengaged from the frantic emotions and returned to the present moment.

That was when the commander finally showed up and told me the details of what had happened and what I was becoming. He gave me another day in the infirmary and when he was satisfied, he allowed me free range of the Garrison. *Get out, stretch your legs, son.*

I requested the leaper to go to the highest point in the Garrison. I didn't want illusions anymore, I wanted something real. I wanted to feel the wind and sun.

No more tricks. Please.

I STOOD in an alcove five hundred feet up the Garrison's cliff. I had never seen it from that vantage point. Bitter wind circled into the opening. I put my toe over the edge. No rail up here, just me and the elements and five hundred feet to the ground. I was cold and alone.

Pretty much how it was on the inside.

If I took a five-hundred-foot step off the ledge and somehow survived, maybe I could run to the wormhole, get as far away from the Garrison as possible. But even if I could survive such a fall, even if I could outrun the long leash of the Paladin Nation, there was nothing on the other side. No home out there. A butterfly cannot transform back into a caterpillar any more than I could become normal again.

There was no stopping growth. If it would bring back Pon, I would gladly lay my Paladin membership down. They needed him more than me. It was a great loss to the Paladin Nation. A great loss to the world. But there was no bringing him back. Would he even want me to?

He said they were going to terminate my training and send me home. That was a lie. They were never going to terminate my training, never let me return, because I was special. Even among Paladins, I was one of a kind.

I am telekinetic.

I wasn't unstable after all. It was all part of the development, and that was the big mystery. I was hearing future events, too. The cold wash preceded the insights. The precognition was enough to make me special, to send me to the top of the Paladins' power list, but it was the telekinesis that put me over the top. No Paladin had ever moved objects with his or her mind. I not only moved them, I blew them across the room. I crushed their bodies. That was what happened in the pre-Trial exercise. Stress levels built up and I exploded. Spindle was destroyed. They weren't expecting it. Spindle had me beat, and then he went flying. It was like fishing for trout and hooking a goddamn pot of gold.

They weren't sure what happened, so they sent me home. According to the commander, they cooked up a scheme to put me under stress to replicate the outcome. They couldn't make me aware of the plan because it might skew the results, so they concocted a confrontation. And lucky them, I set them up with my colossal failure at the Judgment Day club. Pon behaved like Pike, pretending to be a traitor. He attacked. And I responded.

According to the commander.

Then let me see Pon, I told them. *Bring him here and I'll tell you if he was pretending.* I saw it, the eyes don't lie. Pike was in there. He held the dagger to my throat. He had every intention of killing me.

Pigs go to slaughter.

But they didn't bring Pon to me. *Trust us*, they said. *Pon is no traitor.* But they were hiding something, I could feel it, sensed it in their minds. Even the commander. And trust? They exhausted that privilege long ago. But I had nowhere else to go. No one else to believe. My own mother withheld information from me. Who was I going to trust now?

Another gust of wind whipped my hair across my face, like the world was asking a question: *Sure you don't want to try jumping? You never know, you might survive.*

I kicked pebbles over the edge and watched them bang against the cliff until they disappeared. I took a knife from my belt and unfolded it, touching the reflective steel and razor edge.

I'm one of them. I can be nothing else.

With one long stroke, I cut my hair at the scalp and held a handful before me.

Socket Greeny had long white hair. It had always set me apart, identified me in every crowd. Pon hated my long hair because it had no purpose, no function. But Pon was gone. No matter what the commander said, I would never see him again, even if they produced a person that walked and talked like him. *The teacher is gone.*

With my toes over the edge, looking straight down, I let go of the hair. It fluttered in a thousand directions, swirling and separating like strands of silk.

I cut away another chunk, and another, the hair sucked out and dispersed to the world. The world took. What choice did I have but to give them all of me? To surrender. To accept what I was, whatever that might be. To accept whatever this moment contained. However ugly. However cruel.

Life, as it is, the only teacher.

"I have come for you, Master Socket." Spindle approached from behind. "The commander would like to see you."

I cut away the last lock of hair and replaced the knife.

"You look very different," Spindle said.

"You know what used to be out there?" I pointed across the field. "Home."

"It still is."

"No, Spindle. It's where I was born. That's all. Nothing more." I caressed the rough stubble on my scalp. "I no longer matter to that world."

"Pardon my opinion," Spindle said, "but the world is very lucky to have you."

I held up the last lock of hair. The strands slipped between my fingers, flaying in the wind then yanked from my grip like the world was hungry. There was nothing left to give. I wasn't a boyfriend, not a best friend, nor a son. I was empty.

"The world can have all of me."

With my toes perched over the edge, another gust of wind asked, *Last chance, Socket.* I turned to Spindle standing patiently at the leaper entrance, with my heels over the edge. Spindle tilted his head, his faceplate void of color. He did not lunge after me. The end was a mere shuffle away, but he gave me the opportunity to choose. He was an android—a machine—not capable of emotion, created only to calculate. Maybe he knew I wasn't going to make that step. He knew I was only resisting my fate; there was no chance I would step backwards. Or perhaps he was watching me swim in the ocean and could not save me. No man or machine could save me from myself. They could only watch.

I will serve the world.

I stepped away from the ledge. Spindle's faceplate swirled with a myriad of blues and greens.

But not embrace it.

We went to see the commander and to chart a new course for the Paladin Nation. One that included a cadet that sensed the future. A cadet that moved things with his mind.

A new age was upon us.

PART III

The teacher opens the door. The student enters alone.
Buddhist proverb

Your past is an anchor that cannot be cut away. Ignore it, and it will drag behind you, snagging coral and rock in your wake. Your only choice is to pull it aboard to sail freely in all directions.
Trey Greeny

21

———————

Flawed

A BEAD of sweat tracked the side of my face and dangled from my chin.

Breathe in.

My feet were on opposite thighs, my legs folded in a tight lotus position.

Breathe out.

I closed my eyes; the stagnant air wrapped around me, pulling sweat down both cheeks. Drip, drip, drip.

Breathe in.

My awareness expanded to the four walls.

Breathe out.

Every tissue attuned to the infinitesimal swirl of electrons and the pulsing essence within.

Breathe in.

Empty of thoughts.

Breathe out.

Just the room.

Breathe in.

Here.

Breathe out.

The walls spit faceless warriors, their deadly fingers aiming for my throat. The evolvers ignited onto my arms. I twisted. Long, blue whips flailed from my hands. Fiery energy burst from the quiet core of my being, waves of telekinetic power hitting the assailants.

Swipe. Roll.

The whips cut through them. Dismembered arms thumped on the floor. Claylike substance spattered the walls.

Feint.

They counterattacked. Fingers extended.

RrrrrrrrrrrrrrrragharaRRRRRRRRRG!

Another subsonic wave burst from my chest. The warm substance of their bodies splashed over me. I dropped to one knee, chest heaving. I felt the last twitches of their lifeless torsos around me.

Except one.

The last assassin was legless, but lifted itself onto its hands. It craned its neck and circled around the room.

The evolvers unfolded from my arms. The enemy moved carefully over the body parts. I closed my eyes and centered my awareness. Sensing the room, I located the enemy's energy and felt it stalking me.

It bent at the elbows, braced itself against the wall and sprang like a lion.

I felt the space close between us. I deflected its arms open and plunged my hands deep into its chest. The torso flailed, the muscles contracting as I brought it closer, leveraging my grip, my arms bulging until it ripped apart. The body split open with a wet, sucking sound, spewing warm fluid.

My bicep was cut open. White and meaty. Blood beaded on the edges, then began to ooze over my slime-caked skin.

"*Mission complete,*" the room reported.

The room was still.

"AGAIN!" I shouted.

The floor quivered. The slimy substance absorbed into the floor like a sponge until the room was white and pristine. The smell of wet clay lingered. Filtered air wafted through the walls, clearing the atmosphere.

I took my place at the center and pulled my feet into lotus position.

Breathe in.

"Master Socket." Spindle entered. "I must insist you rest."

"When I am finished."

"You have completed this exercise twenty times this morning."

I looked at the gaping wound. "And I have failed as many."

"I cannot allow you to continue. You do not have safety precautions activated. Failure could result in great harm."

"How else am I going to learn?"

"Trainer Pon would not condone your methods."

"Don't patronize me."

Pon was gone, but the Paladins and Spindle still pretended like he had simply been reassigned. He wouldn't be available but would instead send orders. And trust us, Socket, do you really think Pike could overcome a Paladin like Pon? *Then let me see him, just one look.*

You'll see him again, the commander promised. *For the moment, focus.*

But Pon never came. Instead his orders were relayed through Spindle, supplying daily exercises. Not for a second did I believe Pon was actually sending them, so I silently became the teacher and learned how to swim. I looked inside myself for guidance, driving myself far beyond the menial exercises "Pon" was sending. I didn't want to achieve the goals, I wanted to crush them. I wanted to obliterate everything set in front of me. I wanted nothing less than the flawless achievement of total annihilation.

"I beg you to rest, Master Socket. You have not slept in three days." He reached for my forehead to read my vitals. I pulled away. He didn't need to tell me how I felt. I had infinite energy, as if something had been released inside. This energy came out hot and angry. Undeniable.

I had never moved more freely. I had to keep moving forward, don't look back. Home was back there. Chute. The rest. *Just don't look.* I found solace in the pureness of action, when I immersed myself in missions, banishing all thoughts. I annihilated the enemies sometimes wondering who or what I was actually fighting.

"There are many exercises remaining." Spindle stepped back, sensing my agitation. "The Realization Trial is near and I am afraid you will not be prepared if you do not complete them."

"I'll get to them."

"Could I send for food and drink? I believe you are running low on sustenance."

"You can leave." I pointed away. "I'll call when I need you."

Colors scattered across Spindle's faceplate as he contemplated what to do. He was watching me burn out, but, just as on the ledge, he did not attempt to save me. He bowed slightly and left the room.

I didn't need Spindle anymore. I didn't need anyone.

I returned to breathing, calming my mind, letting thoughts fall away. Soon the room opened to me and, once again, I expanded into its spaciousness. Silence washed over me, carrying away the heat of anger. Patiently, I awaited the essential flow of life to open in my awareness.

Instead, cold drained down the back of my neck.

It spread through my shoulders, down my back. Voices warbled distantly. Inaudibly, at first. I braced tighter, pushing the sounds away, but they would not be denied. It wasn't what they said that caused the cold anger to flame brighter. It was laughter.

From somewhere across the planet Pike was laughing. He would have me in the future was what it meant. Surrender was inevitable.

"NO!"

I activated the evolvers, lashing whips from my hands, tearing at the air, gashing deep tracks into the walls. I spun, twisted and attacked the laughter that rang all around, thrashing at the invisible voice.

My lungs suddenly deflated, unable to hold air. My balance swirled inside my head; I couldn't hold myself up.

The room dimmed.

Spindle picked me up. The furnace of hate was still burning.

And laughter trailed in my head.

22

A Paladin is Born

"To the Preserve, Spindle."

For some reason, he listened. We loaded onto a floating cart and sped down the dark paths of the Preserve. The clouds spun overhead and cold laughter trickled down my spine. I clamped my hands over my ears like I could stop it.

As we came out of the trees, the vehicle slowed, creeping up a wide slab of stone. We approached the muscled branches of the grimmet tree. They crawled from their holes and perched on the limbs, turning the barren tree bright with color. As we neared, the cold sensation began to warm. The laughter faded.

Spindle walked around to my side and lifted me from my seat. He ignored my order to leave me alone. When he attempted to put me on my feet, my legs buckled.

"You will recuperate here, Master Socket." He laid me gently between the gnarly flares in the tree trunk. "Rest here."

Warmth vibrated from the tree as if the core were alive. The grimmets gazed down, the trunk flares holding me like my mother's arms.

Rudder crawled down and nestled onto my neck, purring intensely. His breath rattled through my chest. Soon our breathing synchronized into long, deep draws.

***

WHEN I OPENED my eyes again, it was dark. The sky was filled with stars. The grimmets were still out, staring down at me. Then I realized it wasn't stars, it was the grimmets' eyes, sparkling with points of light. Warmth rose up from inside once again, hanging heavy on my eyelids. I sank into the oblivion of sleep.

I didn't dream. Sometimes, I could hear the night sounds around me, mosquito wings buzzing in my ear, and feel their piercing bites, but I never opened my eyes. My body felt heavy, like mercury bubbled up from a wellspring deep inside, filling my veins, weighing on my heart, encasing it like a suit of armor.

***

THE PRESERVE WAS alive with birds welcoming the morning when I woke. The branches of the grimmet tree were empty, their purrs vibrating inside. A thick layer of dew sparkled on the trees. My face was damp, the tip of my nose cold and numb. Rudder rolled off my shoulder onto a coarse blanket covering my legs. I sensed the floral essence of my mother's touch.

The Realization Trial was days away, but no one was urging me to get up. No servys floating up the slab with breakfast. Spindle wasn't there with the morning's schedule. It was just the birds singing. The sun rising.

I tapped my cheek for messages. Thirty of them. Most were from Streeter and Chute. They were weeks old. Spindle must've released them. Pon would've destroyed them, if he was around.

The messages played while I crawled down from the slab to the pond below. *Hey, Socket, it's Chute. I hope you're getting these messages. Can you call back, or send a reply through your mother? I know you have some big test coming up and I just want to talk to you. I just want to know you're okay, that's all. And, well, you know, I, uh... just call. Okay.*

I splashed water on my face and stripped off my shirt. My skin contracted in the brisk air. I dipped my shirt in the pond and squeezed out the excess, rubbing it over my shoulders.

Socket, it's Streeter. Hey, where are you? Did they send you off planet? Call me soon; I got to tell you about gear-addiction therapy. Seriously, call. Or have Spindle call or something.

My knees dented the sandy mud. A foggy cloud of emotion filled my head. My face got heavy.

I'm checking messages, Chute said. *Why haven't you called? I'm a little worried because, you know, the way things went the last time you were here. Your mother says you're all right and I believe her and everything, but I want to talk to you. I really want to hear your voice.*

Sadness hardened in my throat.

I wish you would call, Chute's message said. *I just want to hear you're okay.*

I convulsed.

Socket, Streeter's message said, *you all right?*

I squeezed the muddy sand between my fingers.

I think about you every day, Chute said.

I dropped my chin to my chest, heaving like the oxygen had been sucked out of the air, suffocating like I was on another planet. The atmosphere was crushing me.

My hands plunked into the water, sinking into the mud below. My reflection stared back. My hair stabbed in all directions. My cheeks were stretched against the bones, my ribs poking out.

Who is looking back?

"Delete!" I slapped my cheek, again and again. "DELETE IT ALL!"

The nojakk voicemail reported: *Messages deleted.*

I was no longer that person! That was yesterday! *Another life!*

I marched into the pond. The cold seeped through me, numbing the heaviness.

I can't look back, you understand? I just... I just can't.

The water was at my throat. It took the feeling from my skin. Another step, the water crept over my lips.

I'm sorry, Chute.

The chilly water grabbed my scalp. I floated off the bottom, drifting beneath the surface. The water buoyed me in limbo. Life above. Peace below.

My cheeks expanded with my last breath.

Fighting the water that pushes on your lips...

Sunlight shimmered down, flickering around me. Water leaked into my mouth, pooling under my tongue. Tiny bubbles streamed out, finding their way to the world above.

Water, the very substance that gives you life.

My toes touched bottom. The sun was a distant ball blurred on the surface, its light dim and distorted, barely reaching the cold depths where I lingered.

When life calls for you, Mother once said, *you must find the strength to answer.*

My lungs burned.

Let's hope you are stronger than I am, she said.

The watery sun dimmed in a darkening tunnel.

You can't see what I see in you, she said.

My heart thudded.

But trust me, she said. *Trust what I see in you.*

Shrinking. Smaller. And smaller.

Trust.

Disappearing from this world.

What I see in you.

My body, my cells, my being stopped struggling. The dying light was replaced by images of my past. Memories. I saw my father. My mother. I saw Streeter. And Chute. The cold had reached my core. *Are you sure?*

The world was so heavy. I was so small. So imperfect.

Their faces flicked through my inner vision, spinning further and further back, nearing my earliest days. *Are you sure?*

Maybe they were just memories, but there was something indestructible. Something of infinite value. Something that said, *Yes, the world is lucky to have you.* Something that reminded me that no matter what the struggle, there was nowhere to go. There was no place else. There was only now.

Are you sure?

I had to answer. Yes or no.

In the last moments, I pushed off the bottom.

Water gushed into my mouth as I broke the surface.

I inhaled hungrily at life. Hacking and choking, I struggled to the shore and collapsed. The grimmets watched me struggle to breathe. To live.

Were they watching me on the bottom, too? Where was everyone? Mother was never around. Pivot left. Pon, too. And my father, he was the first of all of them to leave. They all checked out. All of them, letting me drown.

I slapped at the water. Cursing no one. Cursing everyone.

Everything.

My chest contracted. Pressure building. Stiffening.

The pressure wound inside my chest, locked and loaded. I smashed my fists into the water and telekinetic waves erupted through my body. Water exploded in a geyser of foam and spray, thumping with supersonic depth, reaching the top of the grimmet tree and raining down. I screamed their names, cursing them for abandoning me. I pounded the water until my knees gave out.

My strength was sapped, but a resolution had settled in its place. I did not choose death.

Live, I would, but not for joy.

I would mourn the death of Socket Greeny, for he was still on the bottom of that pond.

Water dripped from my face, distorting the water's reflection. I recognized the face looking back. It was hard and empty. It had no name. But I knew it.

A Paladin had been born.

23

———————

Ice Shatters

The days went by in a timeless blur.

Not many people spoke to me, leaving Spindle to pass along instructions. He didn't lecture me on the importance of rest; he gave up on that.

He announced when my day of Realization had arrived. He walked to the grimmet tree. I was sitting beneath it, my legs folded under me, in meditation. He waited until I emerged from my stillness and gently requested that I follow him. Energy rustled in my wake.

———————

We went to a room. He left me there, perhaps expecting me to meditate once again. Instead, I called for it to build an environment. The white walls formed an exact replica of the alcove perched high on the Garrison cliff. I sat on the ledge and let my feet dangle.

It was an important day, that day. Invisible cars had been approaching the Garrison since morning, masked by back-reflection, making the space appear warped around the car. Crawler guards crept along the perimeter, running their own back-reflecting gear, distorting the tree trunks as they passed, following each car that swayed in the grass.

A very important day.

A revolutionary cadet would be tested in the Realization Trial today. One that moved objects with his mind. One that might see the future.

Rain fell from the gray sky and the room mimicked the drops with exact precision. It soaked my hair.

Another car approached, this one evident as the rain was repelled by the warped space cruising over the boulders. Crawler guards followed right out in the open this time, their spidery legs gracefully covering the open land, their glowing eyelights scanning the environment. The clandestine vehicle breezed quickly over the field, slowing as it approached the sheer face of the cliff wall. I leaned over and watched it merge inside.

So important.

Mother emerged from empty air several feet in front of me. She called for a personal bubble to resist the rain. Her breath staggered at first. I could only assume it was the way I looked. I'd lost weight, sure, but it was more than that. My energy was darker than ever, like a storm cloud. She composed herself, then appeared to walk on air to sit next to me. Together, we watched the invisible cars float over the field. Some fast, some slow.

She placed her hand on mine. Her touch was hot. Perhaps she was not any warmer than normal. She had attempted to eat meals with me in my final days of training, but I didn't take the time to stop, preferring to get my nourishment from lifepatches and hydration paste. I slept beneath the grimmet tree. When I woke, I trained. No one came to get me. No one bothered me. Alone, I completed my training. All exercises perfected.

I executed every move, every thought, with exact precision. I learned new information by absorbing it. I merged with the enemy, merged with the environment, melted into the intelligence innate in all forms. I became the enemy, knowing it from the inside. I was empty of obstacles.

I am the weapon.

"Ice shatters." My mother took her hand away. "Water flows."

I narrowed my eyes and watched the field. An emotion twisted in my belly, threatening to manifest.

"It's what your father said after he failed his Realization Trial." She was lost in a memory. "It's what he said when he emerged from a three-day coma. At one point, they didn't expect him to awaken, but then he muttered those words and opened his eyes. He doesn't remember saying them."

Oddly, I couldn't recall my father's face.

"This is a lonesome journey, Socket. In the end, you are on your own. But when you complete your realization, you'll know you were never alone."

"You mean *if* I make it."

"No, I mean *when.*"

"Father failed."

"You are not your father."

The rain came down harder. It was difficult to see across the field. The putty taste of the imitation raindrops was on my lips.

Mother placed her hand on top of my head. The bubble around her hand encompassed my head, repelling the rain. She ran her fingers over my face, wiping my brows.

I resisted the rising tide of warmth threatening to move my heart. She kept her hand on my neck so the rain would not fall on me.

Spindle entered the room. "It is time, Master Socket."

My mother's essence mingled through my mind, leaving fragrant traces of scintillating energy. She paused before she left, but there was nothing left to say.

The alcove faded. Even the moisture evaporated from my hair. I stood in a plain white room. "We will go to a preparatory room for half an hour," Spindle said. "Then you will enter the Realization Trial."

I nodded.

His faceplate bristled with texture and color. "Your father once told me the Realization Trial is quite simple. He said there is nowhere to go. You are already here."

"Then why'd he fail?"

"He said it was simple." Spindle paused before exiting the room. "He did not say it was easy."

THE ANTEROOM WAS LARGER than it needed to be. Ten servys hovered along the back and I faced a blank wall with Spindle by my side, waiting for the signal to enter. I could barely feel my body. No longer cold, I hummed. No emotions, no feeling, just *hummmmmm*. I did not fear, did not want. Whatever was beyond the wall, I would face it without prejudice or preconception.

Hummmmmm.

Nobody entered the room to wish me luck. No one called or sent a message of goodwill. For that, I was grateful.

The room was entirely motionless for thirty minutes. I breathed in, out. Did not move to scratch or ask for the time. It was just in. Out. And on the thirtieth minute, Spindle placed his hand on my shoulder.

"You have been summoned to enter the Realization Trial."

His hand slid from me. I took a deep breath and let it out slowly.

"I will be waiting for you, upon your return," Spindle said. "*Master Socket.*"

He emphasized my name, as if to remind me of something I forgot. I took another deep breath. When I was clear and focused, razor-sharp and deadly rapt, I stepped through the wall to the other side.

No going back now.

24

———

HUNTING the Predator

AN ARENA.

The center was flat and bare. Circus-like. Seats so steep a man would tumble to the bottom if he fell forward.

There was no roof, but the illusion of the sky. It smelled like a transformable room. The staleness of filtered air confirmed it.

The seats were filled with hundreds of Paladins. And not just Paladins, but the elite, highest commanders; the most powerful men and women in the world sat expressionless, wearing dark uniforms cleanly pressed and snugly fit with various bands of color depicting the origin of their facility.

None were projecting their presence; they were all there in the skin. All humans emitted an energy—an unmistakable essence—that many called an aura, but now I was seeing it around the Paladins like never before, blazing around them.

The floor was spongy, but the silence was so dense that my footsteps echoed. The closer I got to the center, the hotter the room became. Not a cough or a fidget, the silence was pristine.

My commander was in the front row next to Chief Com, but there was no way to recognize his rank since they were all impeccably dressed the same, their expressions identical. Their thoughts were like the desert sun, pricking my cheeks. Sweat popped up along my forehead. I remained resolute. Still.

What do you want?

It was psychic heat. They were frying me like a bug. I closed my mind to deflect the pressure. I wouldn't survive long if I didn't. If they wanted to see how many punches I could take, then they had their man. I could take a beating.

My mind clanged like sheets of metal, warding off the psychic pressure that drilled through my pores. But the heat continued. I took a chance, closing my eyes for just a moment to refocus, but my mind felt like an eggshell, fissures appearing like spiderwebs. *Ice shatters.*

Suddenly, a cold sensation washed over me, providing an instant of relief until I realized it was running down my back. *Hahahahaha-haha.* Pike's laughter rumbled like thunder.

The floor shimmered. I took the chance of closing my eyes again, to draw on every bit of strength to solidify my mind, to build a wall. The laughter receded.

When I open my eyes, the Paladins are glowing like beacons. Energy beams from most of them in waves. But others almost look pale and lack the pulsing quality, almost like they are lifeless projections. Maybe they aren't here in the skin.

Distractions.

A fleeting motion disrupts my focus. The already fraying fabric of my mind quickly begins to tear. The icy wave returns, along with Pike's laughter. It echoes around the arena. And then another voice joins it. Chute's calling.

Socket! Please, don't go, she says. *You said I wouldn't forget you!*

I'm sinking to my knees but my feet are still on the floor. The voices are still there. Pleading, calling, and laughing.

These are just hallucinations, I'm not really hearing anything. These aren't real. Just focus.

"You will fail, Socket Greeny!"

I spin on my heels, sweat flicking off my face. Someone stands and shouts for real, then ducks out of sight. It's a brown-skinned man, but now he's gone, like he evaporated. All is still again. I wipe my chin with my sleeve. The fabric is searing.

Socket, don't fight, Chute's voice calls. *Why do you always fight?*

Yeah, Streeter chimes in. *Just relax.*

Chatter, chatter, chatter. Laughter. More voices. Two. Then ten. Mother. Pon. Spindle. Teachers, strangers, neighbors—

Socket, are you listening? Chute says above them all. *I need you! Just come withmedon'tleavejust—*

"SHUT UP!" I shout.

Something scurries under the seats, Paladins shift like it's tunneling beneath them. I run after it and point. "I see you! I see you up there!"

The Paladins don't change their expressions. Some of them are still glowing in waves and others are dimmer. Darker.

I finger the evolvers on my belt and follow the gopher around the arena. I'm about to climb over the front row and into the seats to catch the bastard—

"Father?"

I wipe my eyes and look again. My father, he's there, in the crowd, arms folded, staring with the rest of them. It's him, but I'm sweating sheets. It's hard to see, but now he looks like just another face in the crowd, just another Paladin.

"FAIL, SOCKET!"

The heckler is on the other side of the arena. I blink heavily, nearly tripping over my own feet. Someone stands up and slowly reveals his face. His skin is brown. Eyes almond-shaped.

Pon.

I'm trying to talk, but my lips are quivering. I manage to say something like, "I thought you..." And that's it. Sweat is stinging my eyes and Pon is gone. I unleash the evolver and snap a handful of whips into the crowd, their bodies exploding in a cloud of white dust that settles like gravel.

"FAIL, SOCKET!"

Something thumps off my shoulder. A stone rolls across the floor. I activate an evolver shield.

"FAIL!"

Now they stand and shout, one at a time, chucking rocks. Each one utters the single word. *FAIL.* All with hatred, pulling stones from their pockets and hurling them. I drop to my knees to increase the shield's power, but the stones are relentless, thudding like granite hail.

They're all on their feet. All of them except the two in the front row.

I stand.

Walk to the edge. "Father?"

The arena falls silent. The last of the stones trickles past my feet. He's sitting solemnly next to my mother. Arms crossed. His graying hair hangs over his ears and he has a week's worth of whiskers. His eyes are set in wrinkled pockets.

"Do you see the predator?" he asks.

"I don't understand." My hand reaches slowly, like it doesn't belong to me. I just want to touch his face, feel the leathery cheek, make sure it's really him. I'll know if I touch him. If I sense his musky essence, feel his security, then I'll know for sure.

My hand moves through an eternity of space, and as my fingers brush his chin, he dissolves. The seat's empty.

"WHERE ARE YOU?"

I stumble back to the center, stones rolling under my heels. I fall, catching the jagged edge of a rock with my mouth. Blood spots the floor. I pull myself up. I pull myself.

Up.

Pon is standing there. His eyes are black and empty.

Pike's laughter roars.

It's the predator you don't see...

I reach for an evolver, but the atmosphere is too thick. I watch Pon lift his hand.

I cannot move. I cannot—

It's Pon. It feels like my father. But it's Pon. His hand swings in slow motion.

My father. He was my Paladin.

Pon's finger lightly touches my forehead with the smacking metal-on-metal sound of a three-pound hammer on a steel plate.

"Journey deeper," he says, "into the night."

And night comes.

Night stays.

25

———————

Reflections

Downtown.

I don't know how I got here. I don't care.

The market is vacant. Even the vendors' tables are gone. Not a person anywhere.

The streetlights cast a yellowish glow on the littered streets. My breath is thick and white, but I don't feel cold. I don't feel anything.

A stoplight clicks from red to green. My footsteps echo. Inside the five-star corner restaurant, menus are propped on the tables, the napkins neatly folded, but no one is sitting at them. A television above the bar flashes highlights of a tagghet game.

Around the corner, a neon sign splashes electric red light on a fat man on a bar stool. He's staring at me. I go over, the sign going *bzzz-zzzz.*

"He's up there." The fat man points at the door below the flickering sign.

"Who?"

"You know."

"Pon?"

He doesn't answer, just thumbs at the door. I check the evolvers on my belt. Fat man doesn't seem concerned that I'm armed. I stop at the peeling red door.

Bzzz-zzzz. Bz.

The door opens on its own. I walk up the creaking steps; the walls are covered with graffiti. *Ice shatters,* one blurb reads. Seems like I've heard that before.

Another behemoth at the top of the steps, the heels of his boots wedged on the bar stool. He jerks his head at the crystal-knobbed door behind him. The door thumps rhythmically.

"In there," he says.

"Who?" The word puffs out of my mouth.

He does the same jerky motion with his head.

A black fog rolls in through the door at the bottom of the steps. It stops, but continues to swirl, the tendrils twisting and curling and waiting like it's just cleaning up behind me. *No hurry, take your time.*

The man sees the cloud, too. "Too late now."

I wrap my hand around the angular doorknob. It jiggles with a pounding bass, vibrating in my palm, sending a tickling line through the tendons in my wrist.

Music bursts from inside in loud synthesized dance beats, vibrating deep in my chest. *Dssssszth-dssssszth-boom.* Over and over. The black cloud roils on the top step behind me.

The club looks the same, but the crowd is different. They're younger, packed together with their hands in the air, hopping to the mad, driving beat. The bartender stands with his arms crossed, the vivid red light illuminating his white shirt. He jerks his head towards the crowd and mouths the words *over there.* I don't hear anything over the drowning beat.

The crowd notices me, one at a time, as the rumor of my arrival spreads. They're expecting me. It doesn't slow them down, but they're looking. I know them. A girl leans over and shouts, "Come on!" It's Carmen, from my eighth grade history class. I had a crush on her, but she moved to California. She's waving at me, like she wants me to join the party.

Dssssszth-dsssssszth-boom.

One person isn't dancing. I see the top of the brown head ducking behind the ocean waves of the dance floor. Without breaking stride, the crowd parts. Pon has his arms locked behind his back. His expression is hard. So many times I'd seen that look push me harder, challenge me, tell me time was precious and it was running out. But this time the look mingles with something else, something that shouldn't be there. It's a smirk, one that belongs to someone else. It belongs to a traitor. *Pike.*

He mingles into the crowd behind him, getting lost in the hard bouncing bodies. Hands in the air.

Dssssszth-dsssssszth-boom.

I follow.

The crowd cheers my first step, reaching for me, the roar of their approval rising above the music. Slaton, a lanky kid that was in one of my gym classes, scruffs the top of my head. Then there's Jane, my old babysitter, rubbing my shoulders and celebrating with a *wooo-hooo!* Next to her is Albert, a quiet kid that was my bunkmate at summer camp. He never said more than ten words a day and picked his nose when he lay in bed. But he was making plenty of noise now, smacking me on the back.

The black cloud gobbles up the bartender and crystal-knobbed door.

Up and down the crowd goes, sloshing back and forth. They gently tug at me, congratulating me, hugging me. There's Shelly right in front, his blond hair bouncing in his face. He reaches into the crowd and pulls a girl out by her wrist, spins her around and grinds his hips into her. She turns her head. *Chute.* She doesn't look happy, doesn't look sad. Shelly's hands crawl up her belly, over her breasts—

I blast him.

It's effortless, just a thought exploding from my gut, hitting him like a telephone pole, driving him through an endless corridor of dancing bodies, arms flailing, until the crowd swallows him up. Chute is gone.

Deeper I go.

I reach the end. It's the silver podium where Streeter inserted the key. An arching outline is on the wall. The party rages on behind me.

"He's in there." Streeter's on my left. *I've heard him say that before.*

"Who?"

"Your teacher. He went through the doorway."

"What're you doing here?"

"We're all here." Chute's on my right. "You have to follow him," she says.

"I don't want to."

"Too late for that now," Streeter answers.

The thumping fades. My ears ring as the music stops. The sea of people have solemn expressions. The black cloud roils at the far end of the room. *Any day now.*

"You have to follow," Chute says again.

"Why?"

"It's the only way."

She's sad. But it isn't her. Not really. None of this is really here. Right?

I step to the podium. The surface is cold and smooth on my fingers. The podium connects with my nervous system, recognizing me. The archway on the wall begins to glow.

Whatever is on the other side seems more frightening than anything I've ever faced. I don't want to go, but the black cloud is losing patience. It furls over the crowd, obscuring their faces as it advances. I slide my hand off the pedestal.

"Goodbye, Socket." Chute doesn't wave. Part of me wants to run back and hold her. But that's not Chute. The black cloud is going to take her from me.

I have to go through that door.

It's too late for anything else.

I PASS THROUGH THE DOORWAY. It's not a leaper this time. It's a bright, circular room. The walls are reflective, like hazy mirrors. My reflections look back with fuzzy edges. Doors are evenly spaced around the perimeter.

I walk along the room; the doorways won't open. Pon's not here. Maybe he went through one of the doors, but I'm not going to make this into a game of hide-and-seek. Those doors could go anywhere. I turn to go back to the club, but the archway is gone. In its place is a blank space.

I slam my fists on the wall. "Where are you, goddamnit?"

There's a silver podium now in the center of the room. It wasn't there when I entered, as if it magically appeared, identical to the one in the lobby. My reflection is perfectly clear on its surface. I dip my fingers in it; my image ripples. The taste of aluminum tings in my mouth.

And then the podium opens to my awareness.

The room spins like a carnival ride. Data courses through my fingers, ticking through my nerves like grains of sand, expanding my awareness, filling me with thoughts and images. My mind grows out of the top of my head like tentacles. The air whistles as they swing around. More emerge from the back of my head, then along my neck and back.

I wrap them around the podium and smash it into the ceiling. Now *this* is telekinesis. My True Nature. This is what the Trial is about. I've been released from my body. I am pure power. And Pon thinks he can hide from me?

ME?

The podium crashes, its post spiking into the floor, fragments twinkling around the room. I plunge my slithery mind into the podium. The surface splashes. Currents of information surge through me. I let my awareness absorb it. *Become it.*

I'm everywhere, like the multifaceted vision of an insect. There are thousands of virtualmode rooms throughout the underground of Charleston and they're all connected to the room of mirrors. It all starts here.

It all starts with me.

I am the room. I am the conduit. *I am everything.*

The rooms are filthy little prison cells with patrons lying on piss-stained mattresses. Their bodies are wasting away and forgotten. Maybe I know these people like I knew the ones in the lobby, but I don't pay attention. I don't care. None of them taste like Pon.

I go room to room, sniffing with my mind, searching for the one soul I came for, the one that will quench my thirst. I need to find Pon. I can bring him back, I can send Pike away. If he would just stop hiding.

PON! My thought shakes the walls. *DON'T RUN FROM ME!*

The corridors are networked like an ant colony. My awareness spreads throughout. I can taste the foul flesh of the gear-addicted voids. I plunge deeper. It's colder and the rooms are smaller. The voids are shriveled and weak, but I storm past them. Room after room, life after life, I taste them all. And when there are no more rooms, when there's nowhere left to look, nothing left to taste, it's clear to me. He's gone.

POOOOOONNNNN!

The gear-addicts quiver, twitching to life. They moan like babies pulled off their mommy's tit. I feel their cries inside me, but ignore them. They want to go back to their virtualmode life of dreams and fantasy, and I don't give a fuck what they want. I hate them. They're the ones filling me with rage. It's them. It's their fault.

"Come, you shitbags." The walls crackle. "Come and see what you've become."

I absorb their essence, interweave through their minds and bodies until I'm one with them. They'll come with a simple wish. A single thought.

I open my eyes back in the circular room. The podium is shattered at my feet. The reflections on the walls and doors are crystal clear, the hazy fog lifted from the polished mirrors. My face looks back in every direction.

Come.

They cling to their beds. But I have no mercy. If I'm going to drown, they can join me.

Come to the light.

The first body falls through a door on my right. I feel him smack on the floor like wet meat. His skin is gray. What's left of his long white hair is frayed and matted over his face.

"Please," he moans. "Leave me."

He tastes old and neglected. Forgotten. He's wasted, near death, but somehow he won't die. He paws at my feet.

"Please..."

I've got every intention of wasting him, but there's something so familiar about him. His heart patters and I feel it in my chest, fluttering with fear. I feel the cold floor beneath his palms, the sting of air on his oozing wounds. When he moves, it stirs inside my gut like a spear twisting and breaking.

Who is this?

I hook my finger under his chin. The hair falls from his face.

I fall back a step.

Me.

He reaches a clawed hand. It's my voice. "Please..." The word slips from his cracked lips, but I feel it rattle in my throat. I feel his pain and loneliness.

Another body falls into the room and there's stabbing pain in my knees. He sits up, throws his hair back, and I look directly at my face again. Three more tumble in like the living dead and they're all me. I feel each of them, all their pains and fears swirling in my stomach.

I thought they were just voids hiding from life, but they're me. And now I can see them and feel them. I've become them. And now I want them to go back. I want to forget.

"Go." I flick my hand like that would make them disappear. "NEVER SHOW YOUR FACE AGAIN!"

But they keep coming. Some older. Some have longer hair, others missing teeth. They climb over each other, cling to me, tear at my shirt. They wail and cry, each moan vibrating in my throat until I don't know if it's them or me. I don't know which ones are reflections and which ones are real.

Who am I?

I try to disconnect, try to wish them dead, but they won't die. Their hearts thump in my chest.

"GET AWAY!"

A burst of telekinetic energy slams them against the walls. The mirrors crack. I push with all my will and the cracks run beneath my feet.

I push harder.

They have to go back. I close my eyes, mumbling incoherently, listening to them scream, feeling their bodies squirm. One of them steps out of the crowd, impervious to my will. He comes closer. I open my eyes.

Pon.

He's motionless, hands behind his back. Eyes placid. There's no trace of Pike's menace inside. But he's unconcerned about the hell I've uncovered. Hopelessness howls inside me, and everyone in the room moans like they feel it, too. Collectively, we stare at our mentor. We wait for him to speak. Wait for him to save us, to lead us out of this forsaken place. But he does nothing.

And it's all so hopeless.

I hate him.

He's going to leave me again. He's going to watch me drown.

I wrap my hands around his neck, pressing my thumbs into his windpipe. I squeeze until the tendons ridge from my wrists. Pon's face quickly darkens. His eyes bulge, but he doesn't resist. He gives himself to me.

And I squeeze the life from him.

I pull him close to look deep inside his eyes, to watch him die. The pupils are bottomless. Soulless. I feel him with my mind, taste his waning essence. It's not the essence of Pon I taste. Nor is it Pike. It's something so much more familiar. Something I'd forgotten. And then I see the reflection in his black eyes, the reflection of my own face.

I hold him out at arm's length. Pon's face has become my own. I'm strangling me.

I am my own master.

"Don't." The strength drains from my hands. "Don't do this."

The floor crumbles beneath me and I fall. I hold onto the edge but can't climb out. Below my dangling feet is a mine shaft. Its bottom disappears in the darkness.

Pon is back, standing over me. He doesn't offer a hand as I slide from the edge. He doesn't reach for me as I fall into the darkness. And as I slide down the ever-tightening shaft, the light above becomes smaller. I descend ever deeper. Ever colder. And before the opening above disappears from sight, people are watching. It's not the voids. It's Mother. It's Chute and Streeter. They watch. The walls cave in around me.

The earth crushes me. And before the last gasp of air leaves my lungs, I can utter only a word. It's the single word that I heard myself mutter in a cold dream weeks earlier. A word that seems stuck inside.

Help.

26

———————

Reborn

THE HOLE IS A FUNNEL. The deeper I sink, the tighter it becomes. There is no hope. Only sinking.

And pain.

Slimy mud shoots up my nostrils and packs my sinuses. It courses down my throat and fills my mouth. There's no space to gag, no way to puke the fluid forced into my stomach, into my ears.

Things snap. Muscles tear. If there was space to wish for death, for unconsciousness, I would've called for it, cried for it, begged for it, but I know only agony. There's no escape. No way out.

Falling. Forever. And ever.

Open, a voice calls.

No. I won't open, not to this torment. I won't allow this misery. I fought all my life. I'll resist to the end.

But what if there is no end?

I have to get out, back to the top. Mother's up there; she saw me slip into this trap. She has to be digging after me. I just need to give her space to find me, to pull me out, to take me back to where I was. The way I was.

I pull my awareness inward. What's left of my flesh I could pull to the surface, we could still save it, we could rebuild it just like it was. I just need space. I focus inward and find the timeslicing spark glittering brightly. It's smaller and brighter than ever. I wrap my awareness around it and call on its power. When every bit of me is pulled inside, I pull it tighter still. I'll blow the earth away. I will escape.

Allow, the voice says.

NO! There is no space for allowing! I need to escape the pain!

I release the pressure of telekinetic energy quaking inside the timeslicing spark, and sonic waves rumble through the planet. They'd feel it in Australia, at the bottom of the ocean and the top of Everest. The force will trigger landslides and tsunamis, the universe will feel my wrath. I'll destroy in the name of freedom.

But light doesn't shine from above.

In one cascading moment of utter annihilation, my body is completely crushed. My organs spew. My cries are lost in the silence of obliteration.

And yet, death does not come.

I remain fully aware, buried alive. My body couldn't be functioning, yet I feel every nerve. I feel the burning suffocation of my lungs and the crushing pain. Utter devastation. There are no boundaries to my body anymore, yet I can't escape it. Every thought of struggle, each movement of resistance flares with fiery agony. And every thought of escape brings more pain.

More weight.

More hurt.

(Sob.)

My cries echo throughout eternity, throughout all that has been and all that ever will be. It brings impressions and memories, flavors of my past; fleeting images of my youth scroll past. Each episode carries its own flavor. Some bitter, others sweet. As I experience each one, they release their energy, revealing their essence.

The mirrors are clear.

I am complete.

I see clearly.

Listen, the voice says.

I listen. I open.

I allow.

I begin to thaw, percolating through the earth's pore space, trickling deeper, filtered of impurities, finding the resting aquifer of my True Nature.

Water flows. The essence of bitter sadness transforms into sweetness. I expand, no longer my body because I no longer exist. *Being* is my body. *Existence* my True Nature.

I expand until thoughts are no longer. There is just being.

I just am.

Humming in the great, endless void of space.

Galaxies emerge in spinning wheels. Planets, stars, black holes and light spread out before me. I'm not separate from them, I am them. I can traverse the entire plane of existence simultaneously because I'm not separate from anything.

All the possible pasts and all possible future events exist in the present moment. The future paths spread out like endless veins on the fabric of existence. I could return to any path of my choosing.

Come.

The voice calls from everywhere. Calling me back from another dimension. Yet, if I want to stay in this blissful moment, I can remain for eternity. But something draws me to follow.

I answer. *Yes.*

My answer rings through the heavens. The stars sparkle with renewed life, like points poked through a dark cloth. I recede from the endless expansion of knowing, focusing into a point in space and time.

There is earth below my feet.

A coyote calls.

I raise my hand.

A fire burns within a ring of stones, illuminating cacti and desert.

Beyond the light, in the fringe of darkness, is a man. His hair is long. I can't see his face, but I know his presence. *Pivot.*

It was his voice guiding me, willing me to open and allow. To come.

Another figure emerges next to him. His silhouette is unfamiliar, but not his essence. I know this man, too. I have known him all my life. This man steps into the light. His face is unshaven and a familiar smile lights his face. It's a smile that's not on his lips, but in his eyes.

"Hello, son," my father says.

27

The Last Resolve

THE FIRE POPPED BETWEEN US. Orange light danced across my father's face, casting deep lines at the corners of his mouth. He pushed his hand through his hair and let the gray locks filter between his fingers. Something swelled inside me.

He stretched out his arms. His nostrils flared as he drew in the cool, dry air. He paced away with a familiar hitch in his left leg and gazed at the full moon. I can't see his face, but he was studying the craters on its surface. I suddenly remembered how we were in the backyard and he told me how the moon rotated around the planet and the same side always faced us, that we never saw the dark side.

"I know what you're thinking," he said, his voice scratchy. "Where the hell are we?"

The fire was getting hot. I sat down on a boulder, suddenly weak. He remained at dark's edge, breathing like he missed the simple act of breathing.

"Do you know what happened?" he asked.

It felt like a dream, but if it was a dream, then I was totally awake.

Would that still be a dream? I rested my elbows on my knees and recalled for him the sequence of events, as much for me as for him.

He came back to the fire. "So where are you now?"

I felt the soft rub of my fingertips and the desert night on the back of my neck. "This isn't my skin."

"That's right."

"Your physical body is on the floor of the arena," he said. "They forced you into a timeslice, and while it seems like you were buried in that hole for eternity, about an hour has passed. But the clock is ticking, son."

He rubbed his whiskers and it sounded like a steel brush.

"They've been watching you journey through this insanity. They've looked inside your mind and observed your struggle, your resistance. In most cases, the Trial would be over by now, but Pivot brought you here."

"But why?"

"You've got one last resolve."

He scratched at the whiskers again and gazed into the fire, allowing the moment to stretch out. Pivot was still out in the dark.

"You're not real," I said. "You died. I'm dreaming you like all the rest of this trial. You're a hallucination."

"Correct."

"Then what's to resolve?"

He grunted, which was part laugh, part acknowledgement. The firelight flickered in his eyes.

"Most of what we assume is reality is our own thoughts, our unresolved emotions, our lack of understanding. That's what the Realization Trial is about, purging your depths, exposing your soul. There can be no preconceived notions about what it's about. You cannot prepare for it, you can only be open. You arrive naked and journey into the mind."

"Into the night," I muttered.

"For some, the depth of the soul is very dark."

My thoughts became real. I couldn't escape them. The more I fought the hole, the deeper I sank, the more I was lost. I was crushed under my own delusions and forced to understand. To die. *To be reborn.*

"You see clearly now," he said. "And it comes with immense power, strength and fearlessness."

"I wasn't afraid to begin with."

His laughter echoed deep into the canyon. "Fear has many faces, my son! Anger is just one. The Paladins held up a mirror for you to see."

"Is that what you are? A reflection?"

"I'm a bit more than that."

"Then what?"

He half turned to Pivot. His expression softened, sadness taking the edges off his wrinkles. "You see, Pivot absorbed all my memories when I died, I suppose for this very event to take place. I walk, I talk, I act just like your father, but basically I'm a program." He rubbed his thick, callused hands in front of the fire. "So no, I'm not real. I'm more like a ghost."

"You're data."

"That's another way of putting it."

"You remember Streeter?"

"Your best friend? He was about as tall as a stump and just as wide." He chuckled to himself. "How is good ole Streeter?"

"Never mind." I didn't want to talk about Streeter and the virtualmode trip to see his parents. This was getting way too real for me. Data or not.

"Before you return to physical reality, you have one last obstacle to resolve. Not all cadets survive the Trial, son. Many of us weren't capable of letting go of our beliefs and thoughts." The fire tossed out a streaking ember. "You have one last attachment."

The swelling hiccupped in my chest, spreading outward. "I've seen the ugly, rotting images of myself. I faced them and reclaimed them. There's nothing left."

"Ah, yes. There's still one more." A smile and a sparkle told me it was standing in front of me. "Pivot felt you needed this last one to be special. It's a tough one."

"But you're not real, and you know that. I went through hell back in that hole and, to be honest, I'm not feeling like there's anything left. I mean, you died and that's that."

He dipped his head. The authenticity of the expression was chilling, but my chest was warm. Something was growing. The experience of omnipresence was missing.

"I'm as real to you as I need to be."

"I barely remember you." Something twisted in my stomach and I resisted letting it in, but the instinct to open to it, to be with it, took over and I felt it ache. The swelling entered my chest.

My father looked at the stars, searching the constellations. When the right thought hit him, he said, "You still got that scar behind your ear?"

I touched the raised line behind my right ear.

"I pushed you too high on a swing set when you were three, cut you open on the chain. You bled like a water hose. I caught ten degrees of hell from your mother for that."

The memory crossed my mind. I was telling him to push me higher. Nothing could hurt me. His powerful hands were on my back and sent a fluttering buzz through me each time he shoved. I soared to the peak of the swing set, gripping the chains tight enough to dent my palms, and for a second, I was weightless. I laughed and screamed, *Higher, go higher, Dad.* My father would say, *Oh, higher still, huh?* And then I felt it again, his hands on my back and a sudden surge of power.

The swelling flooded my throat.

"You want my favorite memory?" He shook his head and looked up. "They had this ride at the fair that shot five hundred feet off the ground. You were too young to go, but you went anyway. You were so scared I thought you were going to squeeze my kidneys out." He watched the fire, his expression still. "I liked being there for you, son. It wasn't the ride or the other stuff, it was just being there. That's my favorite part."

Suddenly, I was losing track of what was real again. I knew I was in front of a fire and my skin was somewhere on Earth, but now I was watching my father laugh. I remembered his face when I was young. He was always unshaven. Mother liked that about him, always a little rough and unpredictable. So did I.

I remembered him at the fair. We were eating fried food and my father was holding my mother's hand like they were teenagers, their hands swinging between them. She was laughing. He was, too. But then the memory transformed into a rainy day and he was lying in a coffin and Paladins were lowering him into the ground. Drizzle beaded on the casket lid.

All I could muster was a whisper.

"Why'd you die?"

The fire was just embers glowing in a ring of stones, just enough light to keep his face out of the dark.

"I didn't leave you, son."

"That's not the question. *Why did you die?*"

He looked into the fire.

"Answer the question." The swelling was heavy; it took my strength and blurred my vision. The glowing embers smudged in streaks of light as my eyes got wet.

"You left us…"

The swelling sprang a leak in my throat. Emotion gushed out. But I had more words. I swallowed back the leak.

"You left Mother… and she never smiled again. How could you do that to her? How could you… just leave us? If you loved us…"

I sniffed back the snot and blotted my blurry eyes with my sleeve. The swelling was like an overfilled water balloon. It was about to pop, but I just wanted to know…

"If you loved us…" *I've always wanted to know.* "Why did you have to die?"

The balloon broke.

A flood of emotion, warm and deep, coursed through me, releasing the hidden sadness and deep longing lodged somewhere deep. It filled. It gave.

I shook, holding back the sobs, but they weren't to be denied.

Once again, instinct took over and I opened to the essence coming forth, allowing it to flow within me. I was completely helpless.

Completely vulnerable.

The last resolve.

"You see clearly now, son." My father's arm gently draped across my shoulders and pulled me tight. For a moment, just a split second, the essence of my father—his smell and tone—transformed and I sensed Pon sitting next to me. And then it passed in the unfolding of my emotions because I understood Pon had been filling that hole inside me. The hole missing a father.

THE FIRE IS GONE, but the warmth remains.

I'm nowhere again. I have no eyes, yet I see. No ears, yet I hear. I bathe in the deep, pervading love that has been inside me my entire life.

I have no thoughts of returning to my skin withering on the floor of the arena. I could allow it to pass on, and those I cared about would mourn. I envision their faces, but one stands out in more detail than the others. *Chute.* She'd find happiness after my body died. Eventually.

All the possible pasts and futures lie before my mind's eye once again. I allow one path to choose me. I don't follow its future to see where it leads, where it will end and how. I don't ask if Chute is in it or if the world is safe; I only allow it to take me.

Somewhere in the flow of time, I feel my limp body. My awareness contracts, rushing past pulsars, through galaxies and solar systems, racing with the solar winds. Back to my skin.

AN OCEAN CRASHED SOMEWHERE.

Feeling returned to my extremities, vibrating like I'd been sitting on my legs too long. My fingers trembled on the quaking floor. The ocean grew louder as if a wave would soon fall on me.

You see clearly.

My eyelids fluttered. The putty floor was below. The arena.

No salty air blew in from an ocean. No waves crashed. It was applause shaking the foundations of the enormous room.

I couldn't lift my head, but I could see the blurry Paladins standing in their seats. They were clapping, shouting my name, roaring with approval. No Paladin had ever sustained a timeslice of that length without life support.

Be the path.

Servys blocked my view, their rubbery arms slapping lifepatches to my neck that pierced my arteries and dumped emergency carbohydrates and electrolytes and other life-giving components. The sustenance rushed inside like a cool drink, tingling my nervous system. They hovered around me like satellites, tending to my weak pulse, cradling it lightly, bringing it back so that I could reside in the skin once again.

And the cheers went on.

The Paladins were congratulating each other, shaking hands and patting backs. The Paladin Nation took a leap in evolution that day. What new skills did I bring back from the brink of annihilation? How many more Socket Greenys could they create and how soon? Oh, the possibilities! It was a time to rejoice, indeed. Long live the Paladin Nation!

But I brought back so much more than any of them realized. I returned to serve life, not the Paladin Nation. And as my vision cleared and focus returned, I saw the path before me. I saw the light pulsing around some of the Paladins and the dim deadness around the others. It was the same differences I witnessed when the Trial began, but now I saw it so much more clearly.

And understood what it meant.

"Spindle." I managed barely a whisper, but it would be enough. "*Protect.*"

Spindle crackled from a timeslice, appearing over my helpless body. With his legs on each side of me, he was poised for battle.

The most powerful people in the world were gathered in that room celebrating a new era. But they did not see the path. They could not see what was right in front of them.

I will show them.

"Come now, Spindle." The commander's voice resonated above the noise. "Let the boy breathe. The battle is over."

No, Commander. The battle is just beginning.

28

The Turn

The Paladins came down from the seats, still clapping. It was a historic moment. The commander would forever be known as the one that mentored Socket Greeny. He didn't notice Spindle still crouched over me, eyelight scanning. When the commander gave an order, it was followed, especially when it was given to a mech.

But Spindle overrode the direct command to step away. He was assigned to protect my life and to abort commands when the situation demanded it. Spindle didn't ask why I gave the protect command. He only heeded.

The servys had formed a circle around me, like a crime scene, and took turns administering lifepatches wherever they could find an artery.

I needed strength. Every lifepatch was sucked dry. Servys scrambled to change them, but I drained them faster than they could get them primed and replaced. My blood pressure picked up. I slid my hand across the floor. I'd be able to sit up soon.

[I'm vulnerable to psychic attack,] I thought to Spindle. *[Quietly call the servys into tighter positions and be prepared to erect a psychic shield.]*

Spindle didn't reply or ask for clarification. His eyelight brightened with acknowledgment.

[Lock the arena down on my signal. Allow crawler guards entry, but no exits. No one in this room is allowed to leave. Also, give the order to lockdown timeslicing so that nothing is allowed outside the standard procession of time. Everything inside has to remain in regular time—]

"Spindle!" The commander's expression was mildly agitated. "Step down from the cadet."

He would've come across the room, but another contingent of Paladins approached with hands to shake and backs to pat. The commander glanced at me and doubt crept over his face. Why was Spindle on protective alert?

He wouldn't figure it out. He couldn't see, not yet. He couldn't see what I was seeing. He could see the energy around the Paladins, of course, but not the variations between these subtle differences in energy, how some vibrated in waves and others were dim imitations.

The commander couldn't see that he was surrounded by the enemy.

Perhaps the commander sensed something was wrong—Spindle's unexplained behavior and the insatiable rate at which I was consuming lifepatches—but he was distracted. Even if he wasn't, he wouldn't see what was coming. And I couldn't warn him.

The vision would be revealed to all of them soon enough, just a few more lifepatches, a bit more sustenance, enough that I could survive the revelation. After that, my life was in Spindle's hands. *Will that be enough?*

The servys blinked with confusion and began to send out the warning that I was overconsuming the lifepatches. The ground was littered with them. Something was wrong. Spindle overrode their calls and ordered them to continue and maintain tighter formation.

A curious energy buzzed in the room. Paladins were beginning to notice the servys' agitation. They had witnessed hundreds of Realization Trials and probably stood around while the cadet recovered until he or she could stand and be congratulated. They knew how long it took, they were aware of what it was like to recover, and they were becoming aware something was abnormal.

They looked more often, their glances lingering. But it wasn't the Paladins' stares I sensed. The enemy's True Nature was about to be revealed and, somehow, they felt it coming. Perhaps they sensed the room locked down. Their minds quietly scanned for possible escapes, preparing for the worst. They could handle betrayal, but not in this setting. They were sheep disguised as lions.

Footsteps pounded. "This is unacceptable, Spindle," the commander said. "Step down before you are forcibly removed."

Just another minute. I just need a little extra to survive.

"Is this understood?" The commander spoke his last warning deeply.

Paladins now gathered. Spindle's eyelight spun around his head, calculating position. His body posture readjusted as they surrounded us. The enemy, however, broke away unnoticed and gathered in small groups. *Something's coming.*

"What's the meaning of this, Commander?" a Paladin said. "Your servant mech is taking an aggressive stance. I suggest an immediate power down before—"

"Thank you, Captain Dushawn," the commander snapped.

Just a bit more.

The commander's lips curled, about to utter his last order, when Spindle's eyelight focused on him. "You must prepare, Commander."

The commander's hand moved near his evolver. He sensed it now. The room rippled with tension. The enemies had fully positioned themselves in one large group. The Paladins sensed the tension without knowing where an attack was coming.

Or who.

I needed more life force, but there was no time. I couldn't let them strike first. It had to be—

SSSSSSSSSSSSSSSSSSSSSSSDDOOOOOOOOOHPPBM.

The subsonic wave detonated from my core, rattling the floor. It went through them like gamma rays, stripping away their subtle delusions, revealing the enemy's true nature. The telekinetic wave imparted a sixth sense for all to see that the enemies among them hummed with duplicated tissues and blood and organs. They thought with processors. Followed programming. They were imitations of life.

A third of the Paladins are duplicated humans.

The last thing I heard was the sizzle of weapons.

HOW COULD THIS HAPPEN? The greatest race of humans infiltrated by the very falseness they sought to extinguish. A third of them were duplicated. Were we too busy looking to save the weaker human race, so consumed by protecting what we perceived as the less worthy, that we didn't see what was in our own house?

HALF THE SERVYS were gone when I awoke covered in lifepatches. We were overshadowed by the long legs of crawler guards, their legs anchored around us like a prison cell. Outside the circle, the war raged on.

It was a slur of bodies and weapons. I blinked away the moisture building in my eyes just enough to see a dismembered arm beyond the crawler legs, the fingers still twitching like they were trying to grasp the evolver club just out of reach.

I blinked again.

MORE BODIES WERE PILED up and there were fewer servys. I was covered in sticky fluid that tasted a bit like clay. And there was one less crawler. I felt pressure trying to pierce the psychic shield the crawlers had erected. Where were they finding the strength to still attack? *And where's Spindle?*

Another blink.

THE SERVYS WERE GONE.

One crawler remained. And the pressure felt like someone standing on my skull. The bodies were stacked higher. The arm was joined by a boot with a bone sticking from the top.

The crawlers had joined the battle, spearing men with their legs or swiping them in half. My eyes were heavy, ready for another blink. The crawlers were battling each other like titans, behemoths piercing each other with deadly legs.

Why would they be battling each other?

One man moved swiftly through the mob, his weapon blazing as he cut, pounded and bullied his way in my direction, unconcerned with the battle around him, only where he was going.

Spindle... watch...

Spindle was somewhere; I could feel him in the room. He would heed my call, but I couldn't get the thoughts clearly formed. There was too much psychic force leaking through the barrier, shredding whatever thoughts I could form. I reached for a lifepatch, but most were spent. A stack of them was near my waist. My fingers crawled over the slick floor.

The mysterious Paladin was still slashing his way toward me. His weapons clashed with others and shields collapsed under his blows. The crawler guard did nothing. His translucent shield obscured what he looked like, but I could see his brown skin was bloody. I didn't need to see the almond-shaped eyes to know it was Pon.

He crawled low to the ground, elbows and knees up, like a leopard about to pounce, and engulfed me in his shield, relieving the psychic pressure. Sweat streaked his face. His scar twisted beneath his chin like a snake. He wouldn't look at me.

Pon spied the war outside the security of the shield. A small group of warriors was being methodically torn apart. The battle would soon be over, but I couldn't distinguish who was who in the melee. Their energy was too intertwined, impossible to distinguish one from the other. They all looked physically identical, brother fighting brother. Pon remained crouched, watching. He smelled like fear.

The floor quaked. The center of the room began spewing clay. A roar knocked everyone off their feet. The crawlers staggered. A shadow passed over us like a tidal wave.

Pon looked down. And then we were sinking.

29

THE PREDATOR

PON CRADLED ME LIKE A CHILD. The space around us was black and cool; the war faded away. I felt weightless, like we were floating. I couldn't see walls or a ceiling, couldn't even feel the wind against my face, just the humidity gathering on my exposed cheeks and tickling the end of my nose.

Pon's heart beat against my ear, his chest drawing long, deep breaths like he was working hard. His essence burned hot. It was not the same energy when Pike was in his eyes. Pon was back.

Did he ever leave?

I didn't think to ask him where he was taking me. Or why. I wasn't sure I even had my eyes open.

SOMETHING HARD PUSHED against my back. Tiny points of light coalesced in strange patterns swirling with darkness; then I realized there were knobby branches that looked black and the points of light were stars. The smell of the Preserve was unmistakable.

I had no strength to wipe the drops of moisture off my face. My head was against the trunk of the grimmet tree. Pon stood on the edge of the stone slab, looking into the pond below. The moon cast its glow through the tree, draping jagged shadows across his face, making it appear he was wearing a mask. He looked tired and hungry.

Grimmets scurried out of the tree, observing us below. Rudder landed gently on my chest. I was much number than I thought. It wasn't just strength I was lacking; I could barely feel the soft padding of Rudder's feet. He lay against my neck without a word or a thought and shared his warmth.

"They infiltrated long ago," Pon said, without turning.

I moved my lips but only grunted. Pon didn't glance over, only gazed up at the moon. I waited a moment, gathering the momentum to push out a single word. "How?"

He nodded ever so slightly, acknowledging my question, perhaps editing his thoughts down to the fewest words possible.

"When I relocated Pike, I discovered something no other minder had seen. Perhaps he wanted me to see, or maybe he just couldn't hide it any longer. The duplicates wanted us to have him, they wanted him to betray them, to give up their secrets so the Paladin Nation would win the public war, but in reality we won nothing. They were a thousand moves ahead of us."

I wanted to ask *why*. Why would they want to be exposed? Why would they want their secret agent to give them up? But the answer was now obvious: *The game of war and politics requires a chess master.*

"We thought we defeated them." He lifted his chin, exposing the edge of his jawbone. "All along, they were part of us like a virus, silently spreading the disease of falseness."

He appeared lost in thought. I started to form another question, but Pon held up his hand so I would conserve my strength. It felt like he still refused to believe what happened, too. How could they spread throughout a population? It wasn't like we could become one of them. They were more like artificial intelligence that assumed a moldable body that appeared human. They weren't born and fed; they didn't grow up like humans. They were just duplications.

"They," he said slowly, "were converting us, cadet."

He took a moment to let me process this. He tapped the back of his neck.

"The imbeds in our necks were being programmed to produce nanomechs like a mechanized tumor. Over time, the nanomechs would replace our blood cells and organs until our bodies were completely transformed into something that resembled a human. Until we became *duplications!* In the end, we would become the enemy."

It's the predator you don't see.

Our imbeds were nanomech factories that could produce synthetic white blood cells and repair nerve damage with manufactured connections. We had duplicating technology inside us! *Am I still completely human? Would I know if I wasn't?*

"Why didn't the commander do anything?"

"I didn't tell him," he said. "I didn't tell anyone."

"Why would you do that?"

"It wouldn't have mattered. They needed to see the truth for themselves."

"They would've listened."

"The Garrison is lost, cadet. The Paladin Nation is on the brink of collapse. We are the only thing that stands between the human species and the duplications. If we perish, all is lost."

He exposed his eyes for the first time. He could hide from me no longer. I saw humility. Weakness. Vulnerability. He was imperfect after all. He was human.

"The Paladins needed to see," he said, "what they were becoming. No one could tell them."

He breathed deep again, closing his eyes. Rudder stirred on my neck. I could feel my toes and fingers.

"When I learned this from Pike, I returned to force your telekinetic response the only way possible," Pon said, speaking to the moon again. "I put you under duress, destroyed your identity, and exposed your true nature. I had to bring your powers forth, for it was you that would give them the sight. You weren't ready for such knowledge, but time was not on our side. I betrayed you."

"I saw Pike in you."

"You saw my knowledge." He looked at me. "You mistook it for Pike. But the commander secretly believed I betrayed you. He believed I was sent to assassinate you, that I was a traitor. He sent minders to bore through my mind, seeking information about the enemy. I would've done the same, but he was not aware that the very minders he sent to harvest my thoughts were the exact enemies he sought to expose."

Muscles flexed along his jaw. His eyes revealed the psychic agony he'd endured. His essence was faint, like color bleached from the sun. There wasn't much left of him. They had drained him to find out what he knew. Only a shadow of a great warrior remained.

"The enemy has been waiting for you, cadet."

"Why me?"

"You are the telekinetic one. They would replicate your DNA and quietly infuse Paladins with self-replicating code by stamping it into the imbeds."

He rubbed the back of his neck. I would've done the same.

"But they did not expect you to bring forth the vision."

I shut my eyes. What good was I, lying catatonic on the rock? All the power in the world couldn't save us now; what good was the ability to see clearly? I had nothing left to give.

"How did they win?" I asked. "They were outnumbered in the arena, how could they possibly have won?"

"They are duplicates, cadet. They are manufactured beings that speak the language of technology. What is a crawler, mmm?" He paused. "What is the room?"

They were all nanotechnology; they were scripted programs made up of cellular-sized machines that followed orders. The duplicates managed to reprogram the crawlers and turn them against their creators. And the transforming room! The Paladins were in the belly of the enemy at the end. The floor exploded and a tidal wave was falling on us when we escaped. We were being swallowed by the room.

"We created our enemies, cadet. We didn't see what was in front of us. Who do we have to blame?"

The duplicates wouldn't stop with us when there were millions of humans in the world. Why not give them all an imbed and start the conversion until no one got sick, no one felt pain, and everyone got what their hearts desired?

Thoughts of hopelessness seized my insides. I put them to rest, let them fall away like useless chaff and returned to the present moment. I pushed myself up an inch or two.

"We need to gather the surviving Paladins," I commanded. "Call forth a transporter and get us to a hiding place. Get us somewhere remote; send out a beacon to all surviving Paladins. All is not lost, Pon." I scanned the surrounding trees. We were in the open without weapons or protection. "This is the last place we need to be."

Sensation returned to my legs. I pushed against the tree trunk until I was sitting up. Pon gazed back at the moon, breathing deep, like my father had, relishing the moment and not the least concerned our tactical position was horrible.

Rudder urged me to be still. I consumed whatever strength I had just to sit up. My pulse had weakened rapidly. If I had some lifepatches, I'd be in better shape.

"Pivot trained me." Pon was still looking heavenward, ignoring my struggle. "He opened me to my potential. The Paladin Nation thought I would become his successor." He turned to me and, for the first time ever, a faint smile broke the corner of his mouth. "I was only meant to guide you."

How else would he know the underground tunnels?

"Pivot is older than our planet." His tone was louder and stronger. "I don't know who he is or where he came from, cadet, I only know him. And for that, I am eternally grateful."

Pon bowed his head and his lips moved silently, as if giving thanks. The grimmets squabbled. Pon glanced at them. He shuffled away from the edge and walked down the slab.

"Why did he leave? Why not stay and fight? He could've defeated them himself."

"Pivot didn't need to stay." He took the evolvers from his belt and they unfolded quietly around his arms. The palms of his hands were glowing blue, awaiting command.

"You," he said. "He gave us you."

Pon's eyes remained open and soft, allowing me complete access to his admiration and love. Without him, where would I be?

And then the glare returned. The look of steel ridged his brows and creased his forehead. His lips pulled back, thin and grim. He nodded to me, slowly, deliberately, and turned his back. He flicked his wrists and three long whips slithered from each hand, the glow illuminating the surrounding forest. The whips crawled along the stone like snakes.

Several figures emerged from the trees, all dressed in Paladin uniforms. The central figure was tall with broad shoulders, his hair short, nose flat. It was the Chief Commander. Com. The most successful commander in the Paladin Nation. *Keep your enemies closer than your allies, cadet. That way you always know what they're doing.*

Com stopped at the bottom of the slab. His six assassins continued forward, activating evolvers. Pon did not activate a shield. He stood between the enemy and me, completely vulnerable.

Brute force is the weakest response. But sometimes, it is the only option.

30

THE CALL

It was a beautiful battle.

They surrounded him, each engulfed in a glowing shield. There was no need to slice time; they were all capable of matching each other's skill. They fought in ordinary time, as if the showdown was merely a ritual. Six to one, the fight was a formality. The ending wouldn't be a surprise. Pon took the center.

They raised their weapon hands like a firing squad. Blue pulses blazed from their palms and converged in the center. Pon danced inside a furious storm of electrical whips, deflecting the impossible. The enemy stopped firing in order to power up their shields to block the energy Pon was deflecting back, and in that moment he clapped his hands together. A lance emerged and spiked one of them between the eyes, the two-handed weapon too much for his shield.

The remaining enemies repositioned, allowing Pon to return to the center in ceremonial fashion. They aborted firing pulsars, instead charging with a variety of weapons. They came at him with staves and swords and scorching whips. He couldn't guard against them all, but Pon parried and spun, simultaneously defending and attacking. The air churned and crackled. Shields buzzed and the enemies pressed on until another fell, this one cut in half. Pon wiped his face as he returned to the center.

Com watched as his men fell.

PERHAPS PON DIDN'T SEE the crawler emerge from the trees, did not sense it creeping close to the ground. It stopped near Com, swaying hypnotically like a praying mantis sighting its prey. Pon drove the enemies backward, but his back was to Com and his crawler. An enemy stumbled. Pon raised his hands to end the fifth assassin.

Com nodded.

One of the crawler's legs darted; its needle tip blurred through Pon's chest.

Pon stopped, mid-strike. The enemies lowered their weapons. In reverence, they watched this warrior slide off the crawler's leg. The evolvers unfolded from his arms. He lay face up, eyes on the glowing moon. His last breath gurgled, but he held it. Blinked. And then it leaked from his lungs. His eyes remained open.

All I could do was watch.

My vision had been fulfilled. I saw Pon's death when I first met Com. If I understood what it was, could I have stopped it? Could I have changed the future, or were we all destined to our end?

I did not experience anger's burn, nor the tension of hatred. I only felt the warm release of affection for a man that guided me to realization, a man that served life and had given his own. For that man, lying breathless and alone, I was filled with love. Pon would not ask that one ounce of energy be expended in regret.

But it was impossible not to want revenge.

Pon is dead.

COM APPROACHED PON'S BODY. The two remaining assassins stood at attention while he looked over it. The crawler jerked me to my feet. My head snapped back.

"Gently," Com called. "We prefer him alive."

The crawler's grip eased, the leg still warm from Pon's blood. Its spherical body pulsed like a beating heart. I wanted to destroy it for blindly following orders, but I could barely keep my head up.

Com kept his distance as the enemies approached. One limped badly; the other's face was half-blackened from a near fatal strike. The crawler rose up and allowed them to walk underneath. Rudder stayed tightly wrapped around my neck.

The enemies looked hard, but their stares softened as they neared. They looked into my eyes, trancelike. Their last steps were mechanical and aimless. They leaned in, their lips moving silently.

"Beautiful," the blackened one muttered.

They were mesmerized not by what they saw, but what they felt. It was everything they dreamed of. When all their orders had been completed and every command followed, the duplicates were still left void of life. They could learn to act like a human, to feel and do everything like a human, but they could never *be*. They would always imitate life. What they felt, when they gazed inside me, was the pure moment of presence.

"Step away," Com said.

The two hesitated, but moved to the side. Com was wiping dust from his hands, staring at Pon's body. "I would rather your trainer was alive, but I don't think he would've cared for becoming one of us. He would've been very problematic, yes." He looked at me. "I believe it's better it ended this way."

"How could you do this?" I said.

"How? Why do you think I'm the most productive commander in the entire Paladin Nation? I make Paladins, young man. Then I turn them into duplicates. They're much more successful that way, I think you would agree."

"You're mistaken if you think you've found another one," I whispered. "Lay me next to Pon."

"You haven't heard my offer."

"I've heard enough."

"We've been misrepresented." Com lifted his hands in an offer of innocence. "It is true we've become synthetic beings, but we think and feel exactly as we were when we were organic, yes. We're still very humanlike. In fact, we're better." He shrugged. *And that's a fact.*

But he said humanlike. Even he knew there was a difference, even if he thought it was better.

"I was once human, very much like you. I was born into the Paladin Nation and trained. In fact, I was very successful in my Realization Trial, so much so that I rose to commander in a very short time. I had a great aptitude. I had vision, young man. It should not surprise you that I decided to convert. You see, the duplicates have been part of the Paladin Nation a long time. You'd be surprised just how high up the betrayal goes. They knew I would be a good candidate because I know what works." He glanced at Pon with a hint of a smile. "And what doesn't."

He walked a bit closer to me. The grimmets squabbled overhead, their movements squirming inside my chest.

"Duplicated humans are more intelligent than their originals, young man. They calculate on levels never even conceived of by mankind. They have the next thousand years planned, and it starts with taking over the Paladin Nation. Do you think any of this has been an accident? The Paladins are a formidable foe, and to beat them meant to become them. Duplicates are the superior breed, young man, like it or not. So when I was invited to join them, I simply chose to be superior."

He stood quiet and very still. Strength trickled through my body as Rudder hummed against my neck, but it only made me more aware of the pain.

"I resisted at first," he said. "I mean, the thought of giving up my humanity..." He nodded, looking away. "That's a big one, yes. But I understood that, ultimately, we *can* control our destiny. Why should we leave it up to chance? Why should we let nature decide what we'll become when we can program our own DNA? We can decide what we'll be, what we'll look like. Cancer? Not anymore. Memory loss? Not possible. I can *tell* my body what I want it to do, what to feel. I am an impeccable representation of the human species, young man. *Impeccable.*"

He jabbed at the ground like he was presenting evidence to a jury.

"You see, even Albert Einstein once said that God does not roll dice. God has laws. Laws? Mmm? Does that not sound like programming to you? And in the end, aren't we all made in the image of our Father, if you want to quote the Bible? Humans are self-centered; they are imperfect programs. What kind of honor is that for God to be proud of, I ask you? If we are truly made in his image, then we need to be impeccable. We were given the intelligence to fix the broken human species."

"You're a machine."

"And who says God isn't manufactured?" He smirked. "He could very well be a machine, too. Yes?"

"I've seen the beauty of existence; there's nothing to accomplish." The two assassins still hadn't looked away. "Ask them."

"Yes, well, you've displayed quite a vision, and we hope to integrate that into the mainframe database. We'll all be uploaded with your existential experience. But indulge me for another moment. What are all humans afraid of?"

He lifted his chin, allowing tension to build.

"Death, wouldn't you say? They're all afraid that one day it's all coming to an end, and no one wants that. They want what they have, what they've worked so hard for. They want to keep that." He clenched his fists. "They want to hold onto what's theirs, don't you think that's fair? They've worked so very hard for their life, why should they have to give it all away simply because their bodies can't go on? Wouldn't it be wonderful to possess your life forever, yes? But you can't do that if you remain organic, young man."

He held up his finger, head lowered, holding the final, clinching answer.

"Nothing has to die. We can all live and live and live. Just think, we can manufacture a likeness of your father and upload his memories. He can be standing here, right in front of us tomorrow! He'll walk and talk and remember you, what's the difference?" He tipped his head back and looked down his nose. "If you're one of us, you never die. You live, young man. Forever."

"Delusion," I said, "is not living. You're not real, and you don't even know it."

"You cannot stop the inevitable. Humans are the past. We are the future."

"But you're not here."

He locked his hands behind his back and took a deep breath.

"It doesn't matter what you decide to do," he said quietly. "The human race will all convert in the end, young man. And, trust me, there won't be a problem. They're already programs, yes? The human race behaves from psychological experiences, blindly acting out suppressed memories and fears. Few ever try to understand themselves. They're not interested in discovering what's real, young man, they're only concerned with what makes them happy. They only *want*, they're not interested in *being*. They're infants searching for a breast." He extended his empty hand, palm up, and said gently, "With us, they get what they want."

"And what do they want?"

He smiled for the first time. "Whatever their hearts desire."

I'd heard the argument before, in a parking lot at the high school with Mr. Black. Was he a duplicate? Com was right. They'd be lining up to convert.

The trees rustled at the bottom of the slope. Two crawlers approached with a single duplicate between them, his suit torn and bloody. Com left his hand extended toward me, the invitation still on the table with his eyes locked on mine. The messenger stopped a few steps behind him and waited at attention, his gaze locking on my face. Com finally stood upright and dropped his hand. He nodded to me. My answer was final.

"Very well, then."

"The Garrison is secure, Com," the messenger said. "Civilians and remaining Paladins are trapped in a sublevel sector without escape.

All communications are contained. Air supply has been cut off. Estimated time of surrender is two hours. The other ten training facilities are currently under siege. Seven have already been secured by our forces and the expected surrender of the remaining three facilities is within seven hours."

"Escapees?" Com asked.

"Twenty-one percent have escaped."

"Twenty-one percent?"

"Trackers are hunting. We expect to find locations of refuge within fourteen days."

Com paced thoughtfully. The crawlers stepped out of his way. The corner of his mouth twitched. He touched his cheek, looking around. He looked at me.

I was supporting my own weight, but the crawler's grip was killing the nerves in my arms. Any effort to overwhelm it, mentally or telekinetically, would drain me entirely. Not even Rudder would bring me back after that.

"I want him taken to an infirmary immediately." Com turned his back on me. "Get a preliminary coding of his DNA; then take him for full infusion. Do not hold back, I believe he is capable of handling pain, yes? I expect the full conversion of Socket Greeny in twenty-four hours. Pass the report to others."

Com's head jerked again, as if a thought hit him like an arrow. He looked at the grimmets. He swung around to me.

"You will become one of us." He stepped closer. "It will all make sense when you are converted. You will understand, yes." Closer. "We all understand, young man."

His expression softened, as did the others', as he gazed into my eyes.

If I had the strength, I would vaporize his ass with a thought, but there were more of him. If this many could deceive the Paladins, how many were still walking the streets in ordinary life? How many Chief Coms were there waiting to take his place? How many assassins on the assembly line?

And Com was right, people were willing to become like them. Ask

Mr. Black. They were all out there, wanting what they wanted. I couldn't destroy them without destroying their freedom to choose. How did I change them if they weren't willing to change? Destroying this duplicate would not bring peace. They were self-centered programs. Of course they were self-centered; they were reflections of their creators: *HUMANS!* The duplicates were perversions of our selfish desires; they were self-perpetuating, a more efficient version of the deficient human.

"Com?" the messenger asked. "Would you like me to—"

He held up his hand for silence. *Twitch.* He had the faraway look again, like he was distracted by an idea. He glanced at the grimmets then to me. His gaze turned from unfocused distraction to yearning. He was caught by what he saw. Suddenly, it was too tempting to keep his distance. He needed a closer look.

Com stopped a few feet away. A child's joy lit up his face. He shook his head like he was trying to break away. He began to lean closer. He shuffled like he didn't want to, but he couldn't stop himself. The experience was right there, in my eyes, he could sense it.

He gently touched my shoulders and continued to lean closer. His breath was hot and humid. His eyes were light blue with streaks of darker blue radiating from the pupils. His sweaty forehead touched mine. Eye to eye.

He wanted to *know* the essence he craved like a hungry ghost. He wanted to grab it, to make it his own. So he raised his hand. He wanted more than to just see it. He wanted more than to just feel it. Have it.

He touched my forehead to take it from me.

A LIGHT BURST behind my eyes.

Com's fingers burned, his mind spreading like a fungus inside me, chasing the experience to make it his. He tried to take what was ungraspable, and the more it eluded him, the deeper he plunged. His mind penetrated through me until we were impossibly tangled.

Shapes took form in the white light. I wasn't seeing with my eyes, though; I was seeing like a minder.

Com was convulsing.

The messenger tried to pull him away, but his fingers were welded to my forehead. He shook like an electrocution was taking place. I felt my life force being pulled through his fingers. He didn't mean to kill me, but he couldn't stop.

The density of my physical body lightened. My heartbeat faded and blood pooled quietly in the chambers. My arteries and veins relaxed. I didn't know where I was, but it wasn't my body. I could see it, though, like I was sitting in the tree. I saw Com still convulsing. My body was limp.

All was silent.

There was a graceful solitude to the event below, moving in an odd, slow cinematic way. Nothing was out of place. Everything as it should be.

The grimmets stirred on the branches. I felt their movements. They shuffled again. Rudder clung to my neck and the rest watched from the tree, blinking their golden eyes. I could feel each of them as individual life forces, their essence a fountain of youth that flowed through my body.

Com fell away. The grimmets watched him. He shook his head. He looked at my body like he was coming back from a dream. Then he looked at the grimmets.

"Destroy him." He reached for the evolver on his belt but fumbled it.

"Com?" The messenger stepped forward. "But, sir..."

He had glimpsed what was about to happen.

Grimmets began to leave the branches, circling above, emitting vibrations, a call not heard by ears, but felt by all. More grimmets lifted off and the call gathered momentum.

Com stripped the evolver from the messenger's belt. It began to unfold but fell from his quaking hands. Com crawled after the unwieldy weapon. He clamped his hands over his ears.

The grimmets called to the duplicates.

"Kill him!" Com cried.

They were calling them...

"KILL SOCKET GREENY!"

...to deactivate.

The crawlers cocked their legs. Stopped.

The crawler holding my body gently laid it beneath the tree and heeled like a dog, answering the grimmets' call.

My vision illuminated in my mind's eye in full detail. I sensed my lifeless body calmly resting beneath the storm of grimmets circling above. The call pulsed through my flesh, through the tree, stone and earth. It was a sound beyond the plane of thought and emotion. It was much more fundamental, much simpler. It was the call of existence, spanning the globe as if there were no separation. As if they were one with the universe.

The grimmets were pure presence.

And I was their conduit.

They swarmed down upon my body, crawling beneath it. Rudder gently cradled my head. The beating of their wings stirred dust and debris, fanning life force and heating my flesh. They held me up for the world to see.

The One that Sees Clearly.

The assassins laid their weapons at the tree and bowed. Com and the messenger joined them, placing their foreheads on the stone. They sought to possess the majestic beauty of presence, but the grimmets' call gave them clarity.

They realized they would never have the being of presence. Humans had the ability to understand their psychological programs; they could realize their true nature. Humans had the potential to transform. The duplicates understood, in that very moment, that they would always be a program. They understood that when they gave up their humanity, they lost the ability to truly transform. They would stagnate in their programming for eternity.

The wisdom of the grimmets' call released them from their obsessive chase of something they could never have, to abandon their futile efforts. Regardless of how perfect their programming seemed, no matter what it promised, their search was pointless. They could never be human again. They could never *Be*. And for that wisdom, they bowed.

My vision expanded and I began to rise. I saw the grimmet tree from high above. I saw Garrison Mountain and the endless miles of uninhabitable land around it. I saw the ocean. I continued to rise until I saw the continents. I rose above the planet and saw Earth suspended in black space. I felt life pulse within it and heard the duplicates answer. One by one, millions laid down their weapons across the planet and bowed. They rose above their programming. They understood. They changed at a fundamental level and heeded the call. Perhaps, in the end, they were as close to human as possible.

My vision continued to recede further into outer space. The moon orbited nearby. And as I sped away from Earth, my vision expanding outward, the moon passed in front of me.

And, for the first time, I saw the dark side.

31

———————

Railroad Tracks

Where did we go when we died?

I knew people had lots of ideas, but they didn't really *know*. Even if you died and came back, that wasn't the same as being put in a box and buried. Did we go to heaven? Hell? Nirvana? Were there virgins waiting for us?

I didn't get any answers. I knew my body was lifeless. And I knew I could see it from above like the grimmets carried my awareness and I shared their vision, but where did I go after that? Wherever it was, no one greeted me. No old man with a white beard or dead dad. No virgins.

There was dark and light. No shapes, just the sensation of dark and light intermingled and dancing some eternal dance. And I was in the middle of it. Dark and light.

Dark and light.

But then there was more light than dark. It shrank down and took shape. Sometimes it became a square, and then it would fade and reappear sometime later.

But then the square of light returned and never left. I felt the confines of my body. And the wheel of time, once again, began to turn.

I opened my eyes.

———

A SQUARE LIGHT was on the ceiling with cobwebs blowing in an air-conditioner vent. I was lying in a bed with the unmistakable presence of my boyhood around me. The essence of my past saturated the sheets and the carpet, the posters on the walls.

I was in South Carolina. While the Garrison was capable of replicating it perfectly (even the cobwebs), I knew reality. There was no way to explain how I knew, other than a lack of separation between me and my surroundings. I just *knew.*

But how long I'd been there, and how I got there, I didn't know. My nojakk didn't respond when I asked for the date and neither did the imbed. Both were dead.

Sunlight streaked between the blinds. I put my feet on the floor. A red ball was snoring next to me. I held Rudder by his long tail like a possum, his tongue rolling in and out. I laid him on my pillow.

My body ached like I'd run a hundred marathons. I stretched and twisted to loosen the stiffness in my neck and back, and just doing that much made me tired.

I sensed a lot of people in the house. They could sense me waking and stretching. I couldn't tell who was out there. Probably Paladins. Whoever they were, there were a lot of them in the next room. Mother was there, too. Her scent lingered in my bedroom. She'd been in to check on me.

I scratched and stretched, and then did my morning business in the bathroom. I stopped at the mirror. I'd lost so much weight and my hair was a few inches longer.

I leaned closer and scratched whiskers on my chin. My skin had aged like a sun-baked cowboy. I was an old-looking seventeen-year-old. My eyes had changed, too. It wasn't so much the appearance, they were still blue, but now there was something in them that reminded me of what I saw in Pon's eyes. There were no distractions inside.

I'd put up and taken down enough posters in my bedroom to wallpaper the entire house. Where there wasn't a poster there was grimy tape where one had been. My ancient iPod with the cracked screen was on my desk. A skateboard stuck out from under the bed, a Toy Machine sticker scratched on the bottom.

There was a photo above my desk of train tracks, long and straight, disappearing on the horizon. I was thirteen years old when I put that up. I'd ripped it out of a National Geographic at the library. At the time, I wasn't sure what was so compelling about it, I just wanted it. It represented somewhere else to me. One day I would follow those tracks and get away from the conflict in my head, the anger and sadness that twisted inside me. Those tracks were my yellow brick road to someplace else, something better.

But there was no *over there,* there was just here. I wasn't any more special now than when I was thirteen. But now I understood that. I didn't need train tracks to get there.

Mother stood in the doorway. She had lost weight, too. She approached and, after a long pause, put her hand through my hair. She worked her fingers around my head, not looking in my eyes. Not yet. She eased into the moment, like she was making sure it wasn't a dream. She clamped her lips tight, brushing my hair around like she was getting me ready for school pictures.

I took her hand. *I'm alive.*

In that moment, just being near her, touching her hand, I knew her. In the clarity of my awareness, where nothing was separate, I knew her thoughts, felt her emotions, and saw her experiences. It wasn't like taking her thoughts; it was just a passive knowing, like her memories were as much mine as they were hers.

She had watched my Realization Trial, and while she could not see the torture I experienced in my mind, she watched my body collapse. She watched it convulse and shrink while I experienced rapid degradation in a prolonged timeslice. She didn't move from her seat, ignoring Spindle's pleas to get some rest. She saw the end nearing for me and felt the devastating pain a mother feels for her dying son.

The servys ushered her to a safe haven when the war broke. And when the duplicates converted the entire Garrison into their command, the servys turned on them. They escaped deep underground. She sat in the darkness while the duplicates were outside the door. She didn't know if I survived. Didn't know if she would.

And when it was over, the doors opened. The Garrison was in chaos. She ran from room to room, where servys lay deactivated. The arena was covered with bodies. The surviving Paladins were covering the lifeless. Mother pulled the sheets off, going to each and every one, but not finding me. In the center lay Spindle's body, his eyelight snuffed. He deactivated himself before he was converted to serve the army of duplicates like the rest of the servys. Mother knelt next to him, brushing her fingers over his textured faceplate, staring at the blank space next to him where Pon activated a trapdoor for our escape.

The commander, bleeding but alive, put a hand on her shoulder. "We need you, Kay," he said.

She was brought to the Preserve. Paladins lined both sides of the wide stone leading to the grimmet tree. My body lay beneath it. Rudder sat on my chest. The grimmets filled the branches, watching her approach. They would not let anyone near me, guarding my body like a sacred treasure. But they didn't stop her.

She knelt next to me, felt the weak pulse in my wrist and knew my heart was not beating on its own. Rudder did not have to tell her that he was keeping me alive. It was his essence that beat in my chest and pumped my blood. Without him, all would be still.

"Please," she said to those within earshot, "bring help."

The Paladins set up a life-support station under the grimmet tree. For three days and nights, she sat next to me. Rudder did not leave and Mother refused to move. They waited until I returned from beyond, where the dark and light danced. They waited until my heart, on its own, beat again.

Those were the things she did. And there was joy in her heart to touch me, to see me standing and smiling back. That was what I knew about her.

———

"It's been six weeks," she said. "The Garrison is undergoing a purging; nearly all technology has been shut down while we search for dormant code that might reawaken duplications. We have to expect they were prepared for this sort of thing."

"That's why the nojakk and imbed aren't working?"

"Yes. And as you can imagine, the public is outraged; they want explanations. The Paladin Nation is keeping silent until they clean up their own house. First, we need to develop testing to assure Paladins are human before appearing in public again."

I pried the blinds apart. No cars were moving. People were walking down the middle of the road. Two houses down, three boys leaped off their porch and hid in the bushes with squirt guns and water balloons. If duplicates reawakened, like Mother said, what would stop them?

"Why am I here?"

"Right now, this is the safest place in the world."

I imagined crawler guards perched on the roof like pigeons, but that was impossible. They'd be deactivated along with the servys. *Along with Spindle.*

"Pon?" I asked.

She paused, but didn't need to answer. She never saw his body at the grimmet tree; it had been removed before she got there. She didn't see him like I did.

"He wasn't a traitor," I said.

"We know that now."

"He saved us."

"He shouldn't have kept his knowledge secret."

She'd spent the last year watching him grind me down, and despised the brutal tactics. I could tell her Pivot had put Pon in charge of me; that he was responsible for my development and protection. That he gave me the ability to become what I am. That he kept his secrets and endured endless torture because that was what life demanded. He did those things so the Paladins would see the truth for themselves. But forgiveness did not come easy to her.

"How did he even escape to come for me?" I asked.

"We don't know much about what happened during that period. The minders that were guarding him were duplicates, but we have reason to believe he somehow overcame them before the battle."

The boys' father walked on the porch and casually down the steps. The boys ambushed him. Balloons exploded on his back. He retreated and they pursued until they ran out of balloons and resorted to squirt guns. He chased them and they screamed and laughed.

"I saw Father." I touched the scar behind my ear. She didn't say anything, but I felt her breathing stall. I explained how Pivot had set up the scenario, that it was some other dimension and that it wasn't really him I was talking to, but it may as well have been. "He looked exactly the same, like he hadn't shaved in a couple days. He even did that thing where he smiles with his eyes."

She hummed in response, that was it.

"You know, I always thought I was okay with his death. We sat around this fire and talked about stuff, and then..." I recalled the emotional swelling in my chest. I let go of the blinds. "I miss him."

Mother was looking at the floor, all too familiar with that feeling.

"What do you miss most?"

"When he came home at night." She leaned against the wall and folded her arms. She was still looking at the floor without seeing it. "Every time I heard the door open, I knew he was safe and we'd have another day together."

"Did you know he was going to die?"

"This is a dangerous business. I never took anything for granted."

"So you weren't surprised?"

She imitated a short laugh. "You can't prepare for that, Socket."

Sadness rumbled through her. I let her experience those traumatic memories, how long ago they shook her like earthquakes. Now they were just tremors, but they were still there.

I gently took her hand. She put her hand over mine. We stayed like that for a while.

SLAP. A red sticky grimmet hit me square in the face and latched onto my cheeks. I backed into the wall while Rudder hugged my nose. He pulled his head back and stared into my left eye then hugged me again, squeezing my cheeks with his hands and feet, then gnawing on my nose. I grabbed him by the tail. He squirmed and wriggled.

"You sleep a lot, you know that?" I said.

Rudder giggled that rapid-fire laughter, so infectious even Mother couldn't help but laugh.

"Are the rest here?" I asked.

She pushed the door open to the front room.

They were everywhere. Sleeping under the coffee table, hanging from the lamp, drinking from full-sized cups, ripping apart magazines and tossing wadded pages around like volleyballs. The rest were wrestling on the floor and kitchen table, climbing across the ceiling and flying around. It looked like the zoo for the really weird.

When they saw me, it was immediate silence, like someone shouted *freeze* and meant it. They looked back and forth, not sure if they were in trouble, waiting for my reaction.

"All I want to know," I said, "is where you're pooping?"

Long pause.

Laughter.

Like the funniest thing they ever heard. They fell off the lamps and rolled off the tables, bouncing on their bellies while the walls shook.

They took wing and stormed around the room like a school of fish and out the back door, torn paper and empty cups rattling behind them. We followed them into the backyard. Hundreds of grimmets flocked into the maple tree, hiding behind the broad leaves.

They couldn't stay quiet any more than those kids down the street. We sat on the back steps and watched an enormous free-for-all on the lawn.

Our neighbor looked over the privacy fence. Mother waved to him. He waved back, mouth open, then went back to fertilizing his lawn. The grimmets made him forget what he just saw. The most powerful creatures on this planet—psychic giants, technological wizards, mental titans—playing like children.

"The answer was right in front of us," I said. "The grimmets were waiting for the truth to unlock them, only needed someone to channel their power. They needed someone to see clearly. All this time, no one knew."

She shook her head. For once, she didn't have an answer. "Why didn't they use Pivot?" she asked.

Yeah, why not Pivot? But I knew the answer was beyond my comprehension. There was a plan out there, and I was part of it. That plan needed me to unlock the grimmets. Pivot was just there to guide me. *Where did the plan go from here?*

"I don't know," was all I could say.

We sat quietly, for some time. There was nowhere to go, nothing to do. Mother wouldn't return to the Garrison for weeks. Neither would I. So we watched the grimmets slug it out. Eventually, I chased after them and they cheered and clapped and wrapped their tails around my legs and tripped me and mauled me. They gnawed on every part of my body like needle-toothed puppies until I grabbed them, one at a time, and threw them high into the air. You'd think that was the greatest thing in the world, to be thrown up like that. When they came back down, they said, *Higher, go higher.*

"Oh, you want to go higher?" And I'd throw them again. They laughed and laughed, their bellies filled with joy.

Mine, too.

32

———————

Ice Cubes

THE WEEKS WENT by at home. The first couple days I slept like an old dog, but after that it was time for business. Mother was taking meetings in her room. Then we'd both take meetings in the living room with Paladins projected in front of us. The tone was somber; we lost a lot of good men and women in the battle. A lot of families were disrupted; children were going to grow up without a mother or father, some both. My heart ached for the experiences that lay ahead of them, like coming home to an empty house or a single parent struggling with loss. Some would grow stronger because of it; others would struggle with the emotional holes left behind.

The grimmets made a mess of the house until I called a meeting and set them straight. They were cooped up, accustomed to a forest to romp around, not this stuffy little room and the backyard. They sat quietly while I lectured them, occasionally swinging their tails or kicking their legs. They listened to my impassioned speech about keeping the house in order. I couldn't believe the words coming out of my mouth. A year ago, I was stacking empty pizza boxes as high as the dirty laundry. But the grimmets, led by Rudder, turned their restless energy to housekeeping and our home became immaculate.

The time neared to return to the Garrison. The Paladin Nation needed every single person available. More than that, I think they needed my presence for morale. And I was ready to go back. There was so much to do. But before I left, there were still a few things left to attend.

I was not leaving my life behind. It was as much a part of me as those galactic experiences of spiritual oneness.

I SHOWED up at Streeter's house unannounced. It wasn't like he and Chute weren't calling every day, wanting to come over. I wasn't physically ready to leave the house. I got winded just taking a shower. Death takes a lot out of you, even with a grimmet breathing life back in.

Streeter's backyard was a lush garden with crape myrtles, bamboo, roses and such. His grandfather taught horticulture and spent most weekends tending to his private paradise. Streeter rarely helped. He rarely went outside even though they had a swimming pool with a deck and a pergola covered with jasmine. We used to swim all day when we were little, even before we could touch the bottom, but then we got older and virtualmode came along and the pool became nothing but an expensive chore.

But when I got there, Streeter was sitting in the sun on one of the lounge chairs, sucking on an ice cube and hunching over a small table. He'd gained a few pounds, but was still a skinnier version of his plump self. And, he was tan for once.

I unlatched the back gate and came up the side steps to the deck. He was muttering to a small gear box on his lap, poking it with a tool, slurping the ice cube.

"That's illegal, you know," I said.

"Ho!" He jumped back in the chair. The gear box and tool skittered to the edge of the pool. "You need a bell around your neck."

I picked up the gear and put it on his lap. We took a moment, looking each other over, adjusting to the new looks. *Had that much time gone by?* He was there when my dad died. He was at every after-school fight, sometimes the only one on my side. But now here we were, remembering what it used to be like.

Streeter shoved the chair back and held out his hand. We latched with hands up, then he pulled me close and sort of hugged. It was the first time we'd ever done that.

"Shit, man," he said, "it's good to see you."

I knew his thoughts the way I had with my mother. I knew how he'd suffered gear addiction withdrawal, how his eyes ached for weeks, how his entire nervous system hurt while he adjusted to being back in his skin full-time. I knew how he carried a guilty weight for the incident at the Judgment Day club, that what happened to me was all his fault. I also knew the loneliness inside him, like a block of ice in his stomach. I knew that ice block, too. Streeter hated it, fought against it, but now he was finally acknowledging it.

He was back. Good old Streeter.

"You look different," he said.

I grabbed my short hair. "It's the shampoo."

"Well, there's that. But there's something else." He moved his hand in front of him like a magic trick was coming. "It's the whole package; you feel different."

"Look who's talking. What, you weigh a hundred pounds now?"

"I've never weighed a hundred."

"You did when you were a baby."

"True." He laughed the old Streeter laugh and nodded thoughtfully like he was looking through me. Chute must've taught him how to do that.

"So, how's things?" I asked.

"Some good, some bad." He tapped his nojakk cheek. "I'm guessing this technology blackout is your fault."

"Sort of. But not really."

Streeter lay back in the lounge chair. "I want details."

"You don't want to know." I pulled up a chair. "It's boring, really."

"Yeah, you're right. Fighting death matches with assassins with flaming swords and laser cannons is boring shit. That's the last thing I want to hear."

"Besides, what're you doing with a gear box? I thought you were in therapy. You shouldn't be virtualmoding yet."

"What, this?" He turned the black box over. "This is just a nojakk generator. You know, there's a huge reward for the first pirate generator to override the blackout. It's like ten thousand dollars or something."

I took the box and sensed the circuitry, could feel the basic structure was correct, but his coding was too primitive. He'd probably make it work.

"I know what you're thinking," he said, taking the box back. "But the therapist wants me to do things outside as long as it isn't virtualmode. I can use the nojakk and Internet. I even helped with the garden, pulling weeds. Believe that?"

"You can't do virtualmode ever again?"

"Eventually. Right now, the therapist wants me to talk about feelings and other bullshit. Mainly about my parents, but there's other things." He rotated the box around and around, like it might tell him the future. "We've been talking about you a lot."

That wasn't easy for him to say. Tension wrapped around him. He didn't expect to go there with his feelings with me sitting right in front of him; it took him by surprise. But he stayed with it.

I said, "Hey, well what can I say? I'm honored."

Over and over the gear box went. He shook his head, looking at the clouds. "You know what it is?" he said, his throat tightening. "It's just, you're not afraid of anything, Socket. And I am. I'm afraid of everything. You fought my fights, were always there, and now I got to do this shit on my own and I'm hating it, man. Freaking hating it."

He twisted his fingers like pretzels.

"Streeter, I can walk through the worst neighborhood in the world and nothing can touch me. Nobody and nothing can hurt me. But I still experience fear. I'm no different than you."

"*Right*. You walk on water and I'm crying in the therapist's office because I miss my mom and dad." He looked away, didn't mean to say that, either. "Yeah, we're *exactly* the same."

"What I mean is just work with what you have. That's all you got, just be there with it. Don't be comparing yourself to me or Chute or the president of the United States."

"Yeah, well, don't quit your day job. You're no therapist."

"Never said I was."

"I'm not so sure about your day job, either. What happened at the Judgment Day club? I wake up, you're gone, and then I hear you got thumped. What gives?"

"Yeah, well, I got distracted."

"You're a freaking Paladin!"

I laughed loudly. "You'd be surprised just how human we are."

He fished an ice cube from his cup. Long pause. "I know you didn't understand my obsession, you know, of having to go see my parents. You being a Paladin and everything, I'm sure you got that all figured out, but us mere mortals got to do things the hard way."

Oh, I understand, Streeter.

"Why, Socket Greeny!" Granny walked onto the deck. "Where have you been hiding all this time, young man? I thought you moved away."

"He's in disguise, Granny," Streeter said.

"I can see that." She rustled my hair. "You mustn't do that, you're like family here." She handed me a tall glass of sweet tea. "Are you going to spend the night?"

"No, ma'am. I've got to be home tonight. My mother's expecting me."

"Well, if your mother's home, by all means." She looked at Streeter. "Are you all right, dear? Do you need another drink?"

Streeter said no. Granny said it was nice to see me and went inside. There was no more fade; people knew me once again, like I reclaimed my former life. Now it was a part of me, not something I left behind. I was fully aware of my entire being, had completely integrated all facets of my Self, and I chose not to fade. I'm not sure all

Paladins reached that level of understanding and were able to do that.

"You going back to the Garrison?" Streeter asked.

"Not for a while, it's getting renovated."

He asked about Spindle. About Mother. About all the cool things I'd been doing. I answered in generic truths, avoiding the details that mattered the most. Someone once told me the public doesn't really want to know the truth around us. They just want to feel safe.

"Any new powers?"

I shrugged.

"Come on." He dipped his finger in the cup and flicked tea at me. "Who am I going to tell?"

I gathered a bit of strength around the core in my chest, focusing it in Streeter's direction. He was about to dip his fingers again when the cup dumped in his lap. He leaped off the chair, brushing icy sweet tea off.

"Did you just do that?" he asked. "Seriously?"

Later, I did it again. Streeter set up targets for me to hit. Maybe I shouldn't have done that, but it was Streeter. Who was he going to tell? I ended up eating dinner with them. We didn't hug on the front porch. We didn't even shake hands, that wasn't something we usually did. We just nodded and said goodbye.

"You coming back?" he asked.

"Yeah."

"When?"

I got in the car and rolled the window down. "As soon as I can."

I wouldn't leave my best friend behind.

33

———————

Fishing

There was more Paladin business that night, but I couldn't concentrate. I'd been thinking about going to the park for weeks. And when the day finally arrived, I couldn't think of anything else.

The shade beneath the magnolia tree was deep and cool. The koi pond shimmered in the noon sun, where dragonflies hovered over the lilies. I picked at the kernels of fish food in my hand, tossing one on the water. The surface swirled yellow, orange and white and the kernel disappeared in the chaos of hungry mouths. I waited until it was calm again and threw another.

Chute was late.

I talked to her on the phone the night before (phones were working, still no nojakks). *I've got a surprise,* I told her. She said just seeing me was enough, she didn't need a gift. I wanted to jump through the phone when she said that, but held myself in check. We'd meet at the koi pond at noon. So I sat in the muggy shade, tossing fish food with a mess of emotions in my stomach.

A young couple walked around the pond, holding hands. I only needed a few minutes with Chute and I wanted this place to be empty. The trees rustled like a wind funnel dropped out of the sky, debris whipping around the swan sculpture then pelting the couple with leaves. They covered their heads and jogged off.

Freak weather we're having, wouldn't you say?

I sensed her before I saw her. Felt her park the car by the road. Sensed her beam with exuberance. Her essence pervaded the entire park; I felt it vibrate in my guts! She was a beacon, a lighthouse of essence that buzzed inside me. I closed my eyes and inhaled.

She appeared at the small bridge, emerging from the path enclosed by trees. She stopped in the sunlight like she stepped onto a stage and looked around. Luminescent and beautiful, her essence tasted sweet. She didn't see me and I sensed the fall of disappointment. I didn't want to torture her, but I wanted just to savor the moment.

I tossed a kernel into the pond. She stepped to the water and watched the fish scramble for it. I stepped out of the shade and she saw me there on the other side. Chills danced on my skin.

There wasn't another moment to waste.

I stepped onto the concrete ledge and into the pond, the water up to my thighs. I splashed through the lilies. The water slowed my steps and the lilies wrapped around my ankles. Chute leaped in from the other side, and beside the swan sculpture, wings spread and soaring, we embraced. Her essence permeated my senses, overwhelming me. We squeezed and shook. No separation.

Just wonder.

I could see future moments. In my moment of Realization when all the possible futures were laid out before me, I allowed the path to choose me, allowed life to be present. I didn't look to see if Chute was in the path. Maybe it was better I didn't know.

"I had a dream you died," she said.

"It was just a dream."

The trees rustled. Leaves fell like a snowstorm.

"Don't go away like that, Socket Greeny. Never again." She grabbed my face with both hands. "Can you quit your job?"

"My resignation's in the mail."

Another storm of foliage fell.

No words followed. None needed. I had loved Chute all my life. Just like the grimmets, it was an immense power and joy waiting to be released, waiting to be expressed. And there it was in her face. In her smile.

And then we kissed. Long and hard. Our warm bodies pressed together, our hearts exchanging beats, our essence intermingling. Time seemed to stop and I basked in the moment, standing in the muddy water.

Wondrous.

Something squirmed between our bellies like a fish had leaped from the water. Chute jumped back. The squirming thing stopped on my shoulder and blinked its oversized golden eyes.

"I remember you."

Rudder wiggled with excitement. I held him by the tail and he continued to shake. "He's a bit excited," I said.

Chute cupped her hands. Rudder rolled on his back, hands and feet up and tail curled around her wrist. "*Aaahhhh,*" she said and stroked his stomach. "He's so soft and warm."

She pressed him to her cheek and he purred louder, his tail pushing through her hair. Rudder's essence was part of me; he kept me alive when Com absorbed me. He kept my heart pumping until I could live on my own and even though I was back, a bit of him was left inside me. Our lives were intertwined, inseparable. We felt the same things, sensed the same things and loved the same things. Chute was now as much a part of his life as mine.

"Is this my surprise?" she asked.

"Part of it." I looked up into the trees and saw the glittering eyes looking back.

Then nodded.

The trees exploded, leaves and sticks everywhere. The flock of grimmets corkscrewed and circled the pond, whizzing between us and around us, diving in the water and skimming the surface with dragonflies between their lips. The fallen leaves whisked off the ground.

Chute threw her head back, smiling and laughing, her voice lost in the exuberant chatter. They brushed against her and tousled her hair. One of them hit her square on the face with a fat kiss, pinching her cheeks until I snatched him off. She spun around and around, letting them, one after another, drop into her outstretched hands. They dive-bombed and circled her, coming together for a group hug.

I could've stood there for eternity listening to her laugh.

"Hey! You're not supposed to be in the pond!" The park superintendent stomped onto the path. He was set to snatch us up by our earlobes. That is, until he saw something he'd never seen before. Still pointing, he was mesmerized by the impossible creatures fluttering overhead. Making him forget what he came to do. Making him forget what he was seeing. He dropped his hand, mouth open.

Chute and I didn't wait for him to leave; we chugged out of the pond, lifting our legs high. The grimmets disappeared into the trees, scratching along the branches and staying out of sight. Rudder curled up into the palm of my hand, twining his tail between my fingers. We stopped on the second bridge and caught our breath. I hooked my finger with hers and Rudder wrapped his tail around our hands.

She watched the water run beneath the bridge. "Are you going to leave me, again?"

I didn't want to know the details of our future. It just seemed like a bad idea because if she wasn't there, could I live with that? But when a future glimpse presented itself, I couldn't resist. I saw the future of our path and knew that Chute would be with me the rest of my life. I saw us together. We were old. I saw us walking with wrinkled fingers hooked together.

No, I will never leave you.

34

———————

Comet

IT WAS months before the world got their nojakks back. Virtualmode's return, however, had yet to be determined. A Paladin spokesperson made an announcement to boos, but public officials didn't condemn them. They didn't say anything. The Paladins were pretty convincing, it appeared, to make them see it that way. I doubted they told them what *really* happened, but who knows, maybe they were changing public relations policy.

The Garrison had limited functionality. The training rooms were just white rooms and servys didn't greet us in the parking garage. We carried our own bags, served ourselves lunch and sat on plain chairs, just like everyone else.

We lost over half the Paladin Nation in the battle and most of the commanding tier. The void of leadership was filled with inexperience, and decisions were slow and heavily debated. Mother was needed more than ever. She spent her time travelling around the world and I spoke to her through projection more often than in the skin, but I could feel her no matter how far away she was. I could feel her pulse inside me like an organic lifeline, and knew when she was well and when she was stressed.

I spent most of my time in the Preserve. Before, when I was just a cadet, no one paid much attention to me. I was a promising cadet, but I was still a cadet. In the eyes of accomplished Paladins, I was a kid. Nothing more. I still had to prove something.

But that was then.

I changed the world; maybe even saved the human race. So now Paladins looked at me with reverence. Sometimes, fear. I stayed hidden, most of the time. I didn't want to cause fear; I wanted them to adjust to the new era. One day, when I was dead, the stories would make me larger than life. But I was still alive; there was nothing to fear.

I would not become another Pivot, segregated from society in my own jungle, reverting to a modern-day Tarzan. I would embrace the Paladin Nation, and, if possible, guide it. For the path called me to lead, and that would require knowing those around me. But until things settled, it was just me and the grimmets.

⸻

"ALL CADETS ARE RECOGNIZED for their Realizations." The commander had come out to the grimmet tree alone. "More than ever, we need to recognize this one."

We need you, Socket Greeny.

When the day came, I reported. It wasn't so much for recognition or fame or to prove all those doubters wrong. The Paladin Nation needed to believe in something. Even though these were highly evolved humans, the degree of betrayal had destroyed their trust. Existing without hope was difficult. They needed something to rally around. Even though I understood there was nothing to hope for, that the present moment was perfect, the Paladin Nation needed something to believe until they could see that for themselves.

I WENT to the Preserve deck where I had first met Com. If I knew what he was then, could all that death have been avoided? I still had a lot to learn about seeing the future and what I could do about it.

I stood at the edge, watching dusk settle over the Preserve. The jungle inhabitants greeted the rising moon. Far away, I saw the barren branches of the grimmet tree. Colors swirled around it as the grimmets chased insects.

If only Pon could be here. I didn't want him at the ceremony, although his expression would be entertaining. *No need for frivolity!* No, I just wanted him to see the fruits of his labor. There were so many that paved the path on which I stood, I could only hope that on some other plane of existence, they could see where it led, that their efforts had not been wasted. That I was grateful to have walked with them.

Spindle stepped next to me. He was the only mech to be activated, my special request. His data was backed up and uploaded to another bodyshell.

"How many times are you going to save my life?" I asked.

"As long as it is required."

We paused a bit longer and listened to the jungle

"It is time," he said. "The ceremony has begun."

"Has Mother made arrangements?"

"All those you requested are in attendance, awaiting your arrival."

Yes, Pon would frown on such frivolity, but I would not waste his efforts. Let's celebrate the moment. Nothing frivolous about that. I looked across the Preserve, to the grimmet tree.

[Come,] I thought.

The colorful mass spiraled towards us. Spindle and I went to the door and, before it opened, Rudder smacked into my palm. Hundreds of wings batted the wind behind us. We walked down a long corridor, side by side, and entered the only functional moldable room in the Garrison.

It was a floor and nothing else, like it was floating in silent space with the stars and planets above and below. A half circle of Paladin leaders stood in the middle. In front of them were the people that mattered most. My mother was there. And, upon my request, Chute and Streeter. The three of them stood at attention.

It was good to see Streeter distracted by the technological wonder. I could see his mind already spinning with all the things he could do with technology like this. Chute, though, she was smiling. Her hair was down around her face and her energy was brighter than all those in attendance, pulling me toward the center.

The grimmets erupted from the tunnel and, for a moment, buried us in the furious patter of leathery wings. They circled the platform several times until they were all present, then filled the empty space on the floor, leaving a path for us to follow. Spindle took a step back and a spot glowed in the center. Rudder swung from my fingers as I made the walk.

There was no echo of my footsteps, not even the rustle of wings. All was silent. The commander acknowledged my presence with a slight nod and then looked skyward. While only a few Paladins were in actual attendance, the rest were surely watching the event from around the world.

"It is with great pleasure," he said, his voice booming, "to recognize the accomplishment of Socket Pablo Greeny. The one who sees clearly is truly a gem beyond value, for he is one that lays the path for us to follow."

He made eye contact with everyone on the platform before continuing.

"If there are any in attendance that wish to speak against the induction and Realization of Socket Pablo Greeny, this is your moment." After a long, silent pause, he bowed his head. "It is an honor, Paladin."

A raucous shuffle resounded as the grimmets bowed in unison, all well-behaved. Their eyes were to the ground, tails curled around their bodies. Mother stepped forward and put both hands on my shoulders. She gently turned me around so that my back was to the congregation. Chute and Streeter stepped to each side.

"There is nothing we can give you to equal what you have given us," the commander said. "For the understanding you embody is priceless. But, sadly, it does not come without a cost."

Mother's hands tightened.

"In honor of all those that lost their lives," he said, "a memorial is launched." A bright light emerged from below the lip of the platform and seemed to be far out in space, a long tail trailing behind it. "May its glory blaze throughout the universe until the end of time, so that they may never be forgotten."

The comet slowly streaked away and we watched it shrink into the distance. Nothing was said. Nothing stirred. The ceremony was for all of us. For the world. For all existence. And then I realized where home was. It wasn't in the Preserve or a house in South Carolina. It was here, in existence. It was right this moment.

I put my arms around Chute and Streeter. Chute laid her head on my shoulder and we watched the comet until it was a tiny point of light glittering through the constellation of the Big Dipper. We watched it with wonder.

We watched it right here and now.

WHAT TO READ NEXT?

The Legend of Socket Greeny
Book Three
bertauski.com/socket

The Paladin Nation is rebuilding.

Socket Greeny is leading them into a new era of compassion and understanding. But when Pike returns, Socket discovers nothing is what he expected, that his life has been planned from the beginning. He is faced with ultimate betrayal. In the end, he won't be asked to save the world. It'll be the entire universe.

The Legend of Socket Greeny
Book Three
bertauski.com/socket

REVIEW SOCKET GREENY!

If you enjoyed this ride, please drop a review on your favorite vendor. It doesn't have to be long and complicated. Throw some stars on it and write *Loved it!* or *It was really, really okay!* or *Meh*.

Reviews make the difference.

bertauski.com/socket

BERTAUSKI STARTER LIBRARY

FREE!

bertauski.com

ABOUT THE AUTHOR

TONY BERTAUSKI

My grandpa never graduated high school. He retired from a steel mill in the mid-70s. He was uneducated, but a voracious reader. As a kid, I'd go through his bookshelves of musty paperback novels, pulling Piers Anthony and Isaac Asimov off the shelf and promising to bring them back. I was fascinated by robots that could think and act like people. What happened when they died?

Writing is sort of a thought experiment to explore human nature and possibilities. What makes us human? What is true nature?

I'm also a big fan of plot twists.

.

bertauski.com

www.ingramcontent.com/pod-product-compliance
Lightning Source LLC
Chambersburg PA
CBHW071148180726
48291CB00007B/2370